MW00368551

Meet MR. BRACKSTONE

William Duff

Copyright © 2020 William Duff
All rights reserved
First Edition

PAGE PUBLISHING, INC.
Conneaut Lake, PA

First originally published by Page Publishing 2020

ISBN 978-1-64628-433-7 (pbk)
ISBN 978-1-64628-434-4 (digital)

Printed in the United States of America

For Jenifer & Mr. Guss

CHAPTER 1

Meet Mr. Brackstone

THE EARTH IS OCCUPIED BY a majority of seemingly unsuspecting prey, giving one creature complete dominion over its own gullible kind. The concealed predator is king in our shattered world. The droves of innocent humankind call to this creature, beckon it to devour and tear down for its own malicious sole purpose. At the dawn of the cell phone age and turn of the century, the late nineties were the worst of times for the small suburban city of Riverside, New Jersey. Although the unsuspecting masses did not know what creature stalked them, the town's own dark secret would pounce upon them like a rabies-infected pit bull attacking a defenseless child.

A horrible time of murder, strife, torture, rape, and abuse infested Riverside's dark corners. The prey? Innocence. The predator…suspiciously unseen. From the shadows he lurks, a modern-day scavenger of the weak, arrogantly considering himself a concealed hyena in a human cloak. From the day he was born, a dark cloud loomed across the small city. He brought an ill omen that would leave its sinful mark for generations to come. He was the ultimate predator of the weak, raised by a deformed beast, outcast by the normal faction of his own small-town fabric. His dementia paralleled the cruel product of inhumane thought. He walked among the fragile town inconspicuous and unnoticed for years, picking and choosing his powerless quarry without detection.

Cliff Brackstone is not your everyday science teacher. He looks the part though: awkward frame and small tin glasses which make his nose look rather large. His brown slight eyes resemble those of a small rodent. Slicked back, black hair gives away his middle-age unhipness. And he only brushes his yellow teeth a couple of times a month. The thing that sets Mr. Brackstone apart from the rest of the pack is his special fondness for his prey: the lonely young girls in his class at Riverside High.

Riverside, New Jersey, is a small blue-collar town founded in 1851 by people looking to escape the trappings of Philadelphia. This historical community is where Mr. Brackstone calls home, or rather, hunting ground. The long hallways and shallow back rooms of the local high school are where he practices his perversions on the unknowing and defenseless. For more than twenty years, he has stalked, hunted, and maimed his helpless prey. One question has continuously loomed in Mr. Brackstone's twisted predator mind: How much longer can he continue his reign of terror over the powerless outcast teens of Riverside, New Jersey?

Mr. Brackstone is the worst kind of predator. Lurking dangerously in the shallow shadows, his existence relies on his ability to be inconspicuous. Only picking off the vulnerable, most timid of victims, he never makes too much of a major pull in the fine threads of the small-town fabric. Riverside High is where he teaches science to a bunch of uncaring little shits, in his eyes. Slimy and diminutive, Mr. Brackstone waits at least a couple of months to pick out his victim. He watches and waits for the one strange little girl at the back of the class, the one none of the other kids show any attention toward. She is usually a freshman, though sometimes there is an occasional upper-class transfer he can get his colorless, clammy hands on. He waits, then with the cunning of a snake, he tears into the poor child's innocence. Sometimes when he feels threatened, like if an unknown friend emerges, a snooping relative, or an overzealous counselor, Mr. Brackstone unremorsefully extinguishes her young life.

For twenty years, Mr. Brackstone has kept up his sick tradition of stalking and destroying young girls. His ego grows larger by the year, and his victims always remain silent, one way or another. After his sixth year of teaching, he was almost caught by a fellow teacher. Jerry Hamlit walked in on Mr. Brackstone kissing one of his victims after school one day. Jerry taught math just down the hall from Mr. Brackstone's classroom and needed to borrow some number two pencils for the upcoming midterms. Upon seeing Mr. Brackstone hunched over a mildly retarded small girl, Jerry confronted him.

They argued for what seemed hours. Finally, Mr. Hamlit took the young girl and left the classroom. However, Mr. Brackstone was lucky that day. The old math teacher had a very frail neck, which was easily broken with just one heavy swing of a school-issued aluminum bat. All the other teachers and staff had already gone home for the night, so Mr. Brackstone took his time disposing of Mr. Hamlit. Unfortunately for Mr. Brackstone, the situation called for him to dispose of the girl as well. He had just started his relationship with her, but he could not trust her to remain silent about what she had seen.

So he took her back into his classroom. He viciously smashed her face into the cinder block wall at the back of the room. Her bloody face bounced against the cold concrete at least twenty times. She bled profusely from gaping wounds across her forehead. Her gurgled voice whimpered and pleaded with Mr. Brackstone for mercy. He lifted her crimson face to his own and kissed it one final time. Then, Mr. Brackstone crudely slammed her sad, bloodstained face into the wall one last time. He battered her mongoloid head harshly, only stopping after he heard the concluding snap of her tiny neck. Her lifeless body slid down to the ground.

Mr. Brackstone cleaned up accordingly, and like so many of his other victims, no one really made any fuss about the missing girl. In fact, there were even some people who suspected that Mr. Hamlit had taken the girl and run off with her. The fact he smeared the nosy math teacher's name along with killing him gave Mr. Brackstone's demented self-esteem a sense of sick accomplishment, even though he didn't plan it out that way.

Sometimes he still goes to visit the old boiler room where he buried his colleague. He even relieves himself on the soft dirt floor where he disposed of his nuisance just to have a good laugh. Mr. Brackstone never really enjoys having to kill his girls too early. That is solely because of the hassle of cleaning everything up. On top of that, having to go out and buy some new clothes.

Riverside High is well-known around the county for being an especially trivial school; it's filled with a lot of low-income citizens. That simple fact makes it easy for Mr. Brackstone to get away with offing the troublesome girls, or the ones he thinks will grow to be strong down the road. The runaway rate is about three teens every year in Riverside, so Mr. Brackstone's victims are just chalked up as another unhappy teenager who took off for Philly or New York. Over the extensive years, he's developed a special technique for taking care of the girls. It's not anything elaborate or well-thought-out though. Honestly, Mr. Brackstone really is not that clever. He simply takes them down to the murky Delaware River, stuffs the victim's lungs with some good-sized rocks and gravel, and then dumps the body in gently, under the cover of night. The Delaware's cold, strong under-tow and wild currents do the rest of the work for him.

After twenty well-hunted years, Mr. Brackstone has managed to molest twenty-seven girls and murder nineteen of them. The ones who are still alive are so weak and beat down Mr. Brackstone knows he will never have to worry about them turning him in. After such a lengthy period of destroying the feeble, Mr. Brackstone has grown bored with the homely, infinitesimal girls he has preyed on for so many years. Like a wild tiger that has stared at a lumbering elephant for many years, he wishes to test his metal. This year is going to be different for him. This year, he is going to go for the most popular, pretty, and athletic girl Riverside High has ever seen. The only question that Mr. Brackstone must answer to overcome his thick-skinned prey is simply, How can he deceive her?

CHAPTER 2

Colette's World

SURELY GOD'S MAJESTIC HAND CREATED Colette Jennings, the physically awesome creature that walks so elegantly in Riverside's city limits. She possesses the long-sought beauty of Helen of Troy. The sheer allure of Colette Jennings is, without question, the reason Mr. Brackstone chose her as his coveted quarry. She is undeniably the most stunningly attractive high school senior ever to grace the halls of Riverside High.

If her parents had an inkling of just how gorgeous she was, they could have been millionaires a long time ago from acquiring her modeling contracts. Her popularity matches her beauty, and she can grab the attention of even the most introverted of men. Colette is the captain of the swim team, not to mention the student body president and three-time homecoming queen. If there were ever a shining star to be protected and cherished in the little one-horse town of Riverside, she is irrefutably it.

Colette's hardworking parents guide her well-directioned morality. Both her mother and father are very loving and trusting folks. Her mother is a nurse, and her father works at the chemical factory down River Road, where most everyone's father works in Riverside. Her boyfriend, Mat Pistone, is the big man on campus, as you would expect. Mat is the captain of the football team, an all-county wrestler, anything that comes along with that type of jock crap. He exudes confidence with every cocky bounce through his doubting kingdom.

Every girl in the school pines for him, and every aspiring Romeo or Shakespeare wants to take what he has.

Mat is not unconscious of his position, to say the least. When Colette isn't looking, he openly flirts and takes full advantage of his fleeting status as the high school stud. His antics are as cruel as any jock-hazing ritual behind the locker room doors, but in front of Colette's virgin eyes, a regular Southern gentleman emerges. Undoubtedly because of her startling good looks and supreme status in the peer-encrusted pecking order, it is what she expects and demands from him. He deals with having to put on a good show for her benefit. Plus, if he lost her, all the other girls are subsequently very plain-Jane compared to Colette's beauty. Being stuck with second-best would never do for his monstrously inflated ego. His hormonal sacrifices don't end there.

Where most of the plain Janes would give it up to him in a heartbeat, Colette and Mat have the typical high school puppy-love relationship: mostly heavy petting and passionate kissing, but nothing beyond Colette's sacred underwear line. Her mother always said she should wait for the right time, and the back seat of Mat's 1988 Iroc-Z does not seem like the most romantic place to her.

Colette's group of friends are not really what one would expect, though. She noticed early on that her beauty was going to be a problem in regard to making real friends through high school. So she decided early on to make friends with some of the not-so-hip kids in her grade. Tom Jordan and Eileen Pierce were both bottom-of-the-barrel dorks.

Tom, an avid fan of woodshop and metalworking class, is seen by the rest of the school as the next, never-to-leave Riverside factory worker. He is tall and slim with an awkward, unbalanced walk that only teenagers can master. Unkempt hair wrestles around his greasy scalp. An oily face exudes his age and gives him more than a couple of monster zits every month. Every day is the same as far as his outfits are concerned, which wins him no prizes with the fashion-conscious Jersey girls that mindlessly rate everyone in the school for their own amusement. His attitude in the hallway openly displays discontent for the futile learning which is forced upon him every day. The disenchanted youth does not rebel against the system like some of the punk rockers or gothic geeks do. He simply dislikes the mindless dribble forced into his skull that he will never use throughout his entire blue-color life.

Tom's curt yet openly careless approach to high school life is probably the one thing Colette admires most about him. On several occasions, Tom missed several days of school, trapped among puddles of synthetic oil in his father's auto garage working on his latest mechanical project, mentally enthralled by the mechanics of an old carbon-encrusted four-barrel V-8. He is a true testament to the forgotten mentality of modern metallurgy, gifted with his hands in an unrecognizable way to his surrounding peer-pressured world. His talent does give him a humble confidence, and he carries himself assuredly through the humdrum hallways of his temporary purgatory.

Eileen, on the other hand, chooses to do absolutely as little as possible in school to call any interest or attention to herself. The overweight teen is more like a ghost in the hallways than anything else. Her heavy build and disheveled hair give her the appearance of a careless slob. Usually sporting an oversize sweatshirt to cover her girth, she takes interest in very little and has no real-born talents to speak of. Other students literally run into her through their gallivanting leaps in the hallway and never notice she even exists. Her status in school is almost nonexistent, and she is as vulnerable as an open wound to verbal torments from her heartless peers. Eileen and Tom are, without question, governors on the outskirts of lonely teenage society.

However, a reprieve of profound social bearings weighs heavy on any would-be social attacker of the two outcasts. They are both very close friends to the one and only Colette Jennings. No one can figure it out. She had openly befriended them both as freshmen. They all eat lunch together every day and have for the past three years. Colette enjoys the true company of friendships. They usually spend the day talking about life and TV shows like Buffy the Vampire Slayer, which is a personal favorite of all three of them. The simple fact that Tom and Eileen are good friends to Colette saves them from an unbelievable downpouring of youthful chastising. They do not cling to her for safety, though. Tom and Eileen do not understand the intricate workings of the surrounding social order. So for no other reason than friendship, they love Colette Jennings as a sister. They would both do anything for Colette at the drop of a hat. That is the only way to describe the odd pairing of these three.

Mat cannot understand her friendship with the bottom-feeders of the high school food chain. He never mocks them or makes Colette feel bad about having them as friends, mostly for fear she would dump him on his ass if he ever did such a typical peer-pressuring thing to her. The only thing Mat knows is, those two dorks would do anything for her, out of pure friendship and loyalty, which makes him happy to have them around sometimes. So he always tries to include them in the activities of the most popular couple in school. Tom has even fixed up his cheesy sports car a couple of times, which is an extreme fringe benefit for a jock that can't do anything but play sports. Plus, Eileen is always good for a hidden cookie or snack bar. Besides the minor benefits, he has to deal with them anyway, considering they are all in the same science class with Mr. Brackstone.

CHAPTER 3

Mr. Brackstone's House

ALWAYS STINKING OF CAT URINE and old wet carpet fibers, Mr. Brackstone's three-bedroom colonial is a science project of its own; the outside of the house is battered and overgrown. Forest-green siding blends it into the surrounding vegetation and hides a good deal of it from any onlookers. The pallid, colorless walls inside the house have only one faded picture of the Elephant Man hanging crooked in the living-room hallway. Slow, leaky pipes make a constant maddening drip onto stagnant piles of old dishes which are only washed when needed. Several roach traps litter the dirt-encrusted floors. His furniture looks like the stuff you'd see migrant workers picking up off the side of the road. The bedroom is littered with old tests and graded papers. Dirty clothes hide the horrendous purple shag carpet underneath. The only thing that looks out of place is the twenty-seven golden-framed photos of his victims on top of his bedroom chest.

The golden pictures are reminiscent of trophy heads on a hunter's wall, each young girl looking more innocent than the next. Mr. Brackstone takes great pleasure in these photos. He masturbates to them on a regular basis. From his very first victim, Mr. Brackstone knew he had started something severely evil. With each victim that followed, the skinny, pale maniac knew it would be harder to stop the urge inside.

At this point, the hunt is the only thing in his life. Without it, there is nothing. He obtains no respect from the children he teaches or his peers. His awkward looks and personality will always keep him on the fringe of society. Mr. Brackstone is an outcast in the truest sense of the word, and he knows it. Pondering his next move, Mr. Brackstone speaks to himself while sitting in front of his golden-framed trophies.

"It's been so long since I started this. Wonderful feelings come back to me, ladies, when I look at your pictures. Your sad, smiling faces, all loving and encouraging me to continue with my duties on this wonderful hunt. I have huge plans for our future. There are interesting things to do and new victims to unearth for us. You will all be famous one day. One day soon…"

Mr. Brackstone walked over to his wooden chest and inspected each picture with great care.

"So pretty, so alone, so outcast. I saved all of you. You are all linked to me forever. Though you don't know it, ladies, this is all for the best. It's simply about survival, ladies. Testing yourself every day, pushing the limits, and seeing how far you can go."

Mr. Brackstone lurched back through the filth of his bedroom floor and flopped onto his crusty bed. The only question remaining in Mr. Brackstone's demented mind was, How far can I go until I am caught? This eventually led him to a bold conclusion.

"I must deviate from this path, try a new type of victim. Not the lonely, needy little girl no one would miss, but the popular, pretty girl that would be a tragedy to lose. It is so obvious. I should have thought of this a long time ago. Oh, what a wonderful revelation, ladies! I must take the ultimate prize this town has to offer…and you know who I am talking about."

He steadily looked at the inanimate pictures as if he expected them to answer his strange demands. In his bizarre mind, there is only one girl that fit that bill at Riverside High, the one his fellow male teachers gawk at from the teachers' lounge, the one the gossiping female teachers coddle and love, the one who sits in his fourth-period science class with her all-state boyfriend mocking his very awkward existence just by being so fucking lovable.

"Colette Jennings. The ultimate trophy, the ultimate justice for myself. But first, we will have to take care of a little problem with our current project."

Mr. Brackstone has a steadfast rule for his hunts: he never takes on more than one girl at a time; it is too hard to keep one terrified, let alone two at once. His current victim is never going to be a problem for him down the road. However, he does not want to leave a loose end hanging in the wind should something go amiss with Colette.

He sat on his bed and pondered his position and was almost strangely upset when he decided he would have to kill Eileen Pierce. However, the soft emotion faded fast into the empty depths of his black heart. After all, she has been such an enjoyable victim, never saying a thing to anybody about their "special relationship," as Mr. Brackstone calls it.

Eileen has always remained the out-of-place ghost of a girl he can take full advantage of anytime he feels like it. He has even gotten her back to his house a couple of times. Sure, she is fat and relatively unattractive, but she is like putty in the hands of a master sculptor. Mr. Brackstone doesn't even know that Colette and Eileen are close friends, or that she has any close friends at all.

Mr. Brackstone pulled out a school photo of Colette that was taken at last year's homecoming. He traced her face with his fingers, fantasizing about his demented future endeavor.

He licked the picture then spoke slowly to the glossy likeness, in a romantic tone, "How can I make you understand, Colette? How can I trick you? You are so perfect and protected... But you will know pain when this is all said and done. You will know why you should look over your shoulder. There is a game that has started, my sweet, and you haven't even realized it yet. A game for your life. I wonder, Will your good looks help you then? Will your homecoming crown save you from what I plan to do to you? I think not, Colette. I think you are going to be my greatest triumph. You will be mine."

CHAPTER 4

What to Do about Eileen

COLETTE AND HER ODD CREW sat in fourth-period science class doing the lab work that Mr. Brackstone assigned. Unaware of the plotting monster that sat just a few desks in front of them, Eileen and Colette were having a hushed conversation about the new episode of *Buffy the Vampire Slayer*.

"I don't think *Buffy* is as good as it was last year," Eileen said with her usual whimper.

"You're right, it's not, but it sure beats all those dumb-guy shows they have on TV every night, like Monday night wrestling," Colette uttered while making a wrestler-type face and flexing her sleek yet sexy muscles.

Eileen laughed. She loves how Colette makes her feel. The way she really listens to what she has to say makes her feel special. Eileen momentarily pondered telling Colette about her "special relationship" with Mr. Brackstone. A couple of times, she even started the sad tale, only to change the subject quickly. The inner morals she fights against to justify what she does keep her mouth tightly shut. Eileen tells herself she will get into trouble, although she knows it wouldn't be *her* head on the chopping block if anyone found out. So Eileen simply acts like nothing is out of the ordinary.

When Eileen is spending time with Colette, nothing seems to be wrong in her awkward life. Colette always cheers her up and makes sure she has something to talk or joke about with her. Even when she is ignored by everyone else in the school, as long as Colette Jennings is a simple phone call away, it does not matter to her one bit. The fear of Colette turning her back on her because of what she does with Mr. Brackstone is an unbearable thought to her youthful mind.

"Hey, Colette, thanks for being so cool with me," Eileen said.

"Eileen, I told you to stop saying that type of crap to me. We are friends. You don't have to thank me for being nice to you. I'm supposed to be."

Eileen smiled back at her perfect companion. She realized a long time ago that it is strange for someone like Colette to be acquaintances with an overweight, underprivileged, very below-average girl like herself. She eventually figured it was God's way of showing her not everything in life is hard and callous. Eileen truly loves Colette, in a very genuine, childlike way. If she only knew what her manipulative tormentor was plotting at his oversize blacktop teacher's table... She would have told every student what was going down with her and Mr. Brackstone right then and there.

Eileen turned to Colette and asked, "Hey, do you think we will be best friends forever?"

"Of course, silly. I will always be your best friend. No matter where we go or what we do. Whenever you need me, I will be there for you."

"You're a really good person, Colette. I consider myself very lucky to have you around. Now let's get this dumb rock lab done before we both fail."

"Good idea," replied Colette as she held up the large dark piece of iron ore. "But I think we are just identifying some fossilized poop."

Both of the girls laughed and playfully continued the tedious lab. Mr. Brackstone sat fifteen feet away, hunched over at his desk, eerily staring at the two girls through his tinted glasses. He prefers to wear them in class so he can look up the girls' skirts and shorts without anyone noticing.

Mr. Brackstone began to psychologically address the issue of what to do about his plump prey, Eileen, as he watched over his functioning class. Her unsightly large form presents a sizable challenge for his diminutive slightness. He knows all too well she is probably just as strong as he is, maybe even stronger, which definitely rules out strangulation. He cautiously brooded at his desk, plotting a million different ways of destroying Eileen's young life as she harmlessly worked on identifying a piece of powder-white chalk for the lab assignment he handed out. He stared at her plump body in horrid disgust. Searching through his manic mind for a way of tackling her sheer girth began to envelop Mr. Brackstone's psychotic nature. In the past, he used many different depraved methods in murdering his young victims.

While sitting at his desk, Mr. Brackstone had a suddenly fiendish recall about the most disturbing thing that had happened to him while killing one of his previous victims. In that atrocious instance, Mr. Brackstone tried to poison little Cindy Chadsworth with arsenic. Cindy was grossly skinny and weak, a burdened child with only one arm. She was an outcast in Riverside High's social fabric and had an extremely introverted personality, probably because of her deformity. The harsh ribbings of her classmates intensified it tenfold.

He decided to put the poison in a pound cake that he made special, just for her. On top of the cake, he wrote, "*To Cindy, my special girl.*" Mr. Brackstone spiked the cake with just a little poison, figuring it would not take much to kill her; however, it turned out he did not use enough. Instead of dying right there on the spot, he was forced to deal with deformed little Cindy projectile vomiting blood all over his clothes and classroom. She tried to cry out and scream, but every time she opened her mouth, more blood and stomach bile rushed out of her as she gasped for air. The freshly digested poison attacked her with burning pain, up her esophagus, and all over her lips.

As she hunched over in uncontrollable convulsions, Mr. Brackstone viciously beat her to death with a classroom chair. He wildly struck her with the heavy metal chair dozens of times, breaking bones and splitting her flesh with every terrible blow. The final strike impaled her fragile face through the eye socket with the chair's skinny, jagged leg. The crunching sound stuck in Mr. Brackstone's mind like a bad dream. It sounded like someone dropped a large basket of eggs all at once. He was exhausted from the ordeal and barely had enough time to clean up the mess before the night janitor came in.

The recall sent an army of nervous energy dancing down his spine. Mr. Brackstone shuddered in his seat as if an ice cube had been dropped down his back. He immediately snapped out of his flashback stupor. Mr. Brackstone wiped a puddle of sweat off his greasy forehead. He had learned a lot since Cindy. A sense of utter determination rushed over him. He realized he would have to take care of this Eileen issue with more savvy than that. Mr. Brackstone passed Eileen a note on an old quiz, as he usually does when he wants to see her.

It read, *"Meet me after school. I have a wonderful surprise for my special student. And make sure you bring your things."*

Eileen looked at Mr. Brackstone in disgust as he handed out the rest of the old graded tests. She did not think twice about the note. She has received so many of them by now. At least one a week, so she thought she knew what he wanted. Only this time, he wanted something Eileen could not have imagined in her most sinister of nightmares. A thought came into her mind to show the note to Colette; it passed quickly. She thought of the trouble she might get into if anyone found out what she had been doing.

So she folded up the paper and placed it in her pocket, not knowing what the great manipulator of children had in store for her, not knowing her silence would cost her the ultimate price and put all her friends in the destructive path of the murderous, vile, and unrelenting savage…Mr. Brackstone.

CHAPTER 5

Mildred Comes Home

FIFTEEN YEARS AGO, MILDRED BERON left the small township of Riverside, New Jersey, vowing to never return and to never talk about what happened to her or even reflect on the place in her passing memories. In high school, she was an outcast due to the humiliating large red birthmark on her face. It resembled a blotchy red mask over her right eye and cheek. At first sight, it looked as if the skin on the right side of her face was peeled off. However, upon further scrutiny, one could see the raised, unnatural markings of a birth defect that repulsed the average onlooker.

The former displaced youth arrived in a cloud of dust and gravel under the tires of her 1986 Chevy Caprice Classic. Looking into her rearview mirror, her stone-cold and determined eyes shimmered at her half-red face with Riverside High School just behind her. Thinking back, she began to easily remember her years long hidden away.

The unsympathetic children at school gave her no social reprieve. They used to call her "Rusty" on account of the rusted-looking color of the unusual mark. Youthful ignorance sent Mildred into a pit of self-loathing before she even reached Riverside High School. She grew up in a loveless home with an alcoholic for a father and a manic-depressive mother. When Mildred met Mr. Brackstone in her science class, he showed her friendly attention for the first time in her life. All the other things he did to her were blocked out or placed in a steel trap hidden in the back of her mind.

He was the first and only person that ever told her she was pretty. If you covered up the rusted mark on her face and truly fixed Mildred up, she actually was a fine-looking girl back then. However, the years of abuse had taken their cruel toll. Mildred hardly brushed her hair then and still doesn't now. The hard lines on her weathered face belong to a person who had been through a tragically poor upbringing. The gentle hand of Mr. Brackstone back in her youthful days seemed like a good thing to her. It was not until she got out into the real world that she realized the reality of the situation.

Mr. Brackstone snared Mildred in a deceptive trap during her freshman year. She had him as a teacher every day for earth science. Mr. Brackstone noticed how lonely she was right away. He diligently invited her to stay after school several times, feeling her out, trying to see how submissive she was to his advances. Finally, halfway through her lonesome freshman year, Mr. Brackstone slyly coaxed her into the back of the science lab. Mildred remembered the incident as if it had just happened to her. She closed her eyes and remembered the first uncomfortable rendezvous. Just one of many rapes...

Mr. Brackstone closed the door behind them and locked it. He walked over and took Mildred by the hand.

"Mildred, I am so glad you could come after school today and spend some special time with me."

"Mr. Brackstone, why are we back here?"

"Well, that's what I wanted to talk to you about, honey. You see, I really like you. Do you like me?"

"Yes, I suppose."

"That's good. That's very good, Mildred. Now we are both adults, right?"

"I guess so..."

"Well, Mildred, when adults like each other, they do special things to show how much they really want to make the other person feel good."

"Special things like what, Mr. Brackstone?"

Mr. Brackstone smiled and ran his pale hands through Mildred's hair. He advanced on her, pressing his bony body up against her soft midsection.

"I'm glad you asked, honey. You see, I really want you to like me, because you are my favorite student. In fact, you are more than just a student to me, Mildred, you are my friend. I want to make you feel good. And I want you to make me feel good too. So would you like me to show you how?"

Mildred backed up against the wall. She hid her chin in her chest and crossed her arms in a naturally defensive manner.

"Mr. Brackstone, I don't think we should be doing this. I am scared."

Mr. Brackstone hurried over to her like a seasoned pro and took her in his arms.

"Mildred, I would never do anything to hurt you, honey. I just want to make you feel special. Don't you want to feel special?"

"Yes, I do want to feel special, Mr. Brackstone, but…"

Mr. Brackstone cut her off midsentence.

"That's what I thought. Now, I am going to make you feel so good, Mildred, you are going to want to come visit me every day after this."

Mr. Brackstone brushed Mildred's hair back and stuck his long saliva-soaked tongue in her ear. He lapped in and out of her eardrum then down her neck like a dog licking peanut butter off its master's hand. Mildred felt a warm sensation trickle through her body. It was an inviting feeling that embraced her yearning soul. She curiously reached around Mr. Brackstone and held him, giving him the go-ahead sign of acceptance.

Mr. Brackstone jumped at the opening with stunning accuracy. He savagely ripped at her clothes, exposing her young yet perky breasts. She wanted to say no, but Mr. Brackstone jammed his wet tongue down her throat before she could get the words out. The feeling of someone wanting her in this way seemed wonderful to an unwanted outcast. She allowed Mr. Brackstone to continue his sexual assault, not knowing how wrong it was. Mr. Brackstone proceeded to remove the rest of her clothes and then his own. He forced his face down to her young, underdeveloped breasts and licked at her nipples until they grew firm and hard.

Mildred panted and heaved for air. The new feeling of sexuality was confusing and scary to her. She did not know how to act or what to do. Mr. Brackstone continued kissing his way down her skinny, quivering stomach. She tried to force his head back up, but it was too late; he had already driven his face into her crotch.

She had never felt anything like it before. She became flushed and threw her arms back against the wall, bracing her body for the strange invasion taking place. Her entire body tingled with a curiously wonderful sensation. She was so surprised by her feelings she screamed out in panic. Mr. Brackstone quickly placed his hand over her mouth.

"No, don't be scared, Mildred. It is only natural."

Mr. Brackstone spread her skinny legs and hoisted her up on the small lab countertop. He entered her harshly, ripping through her youthful spirit, pumping harder and harder. She was shocked at the pain and tried to scream out once more, but Mr. Brackstone rammed his tongue into her cavernous mouth to prevent any noise. He thrust in quick and deep. His unsightly body poured sweat down Mildred's shaking nude skin. He engulfed her in his intense animalistic behavior.

Mr. Brackstone's eyes became unrecognizable, like a wild animal that had been chained for the first time. He squealed and moaned until, finally, he made a grotesque face and finished his tawdry deed inside her. Mildred held on to her teacher tightly.

Confused and frightened, she gave in to his demands time and again. In her mind, it was better than being alone all the time. The abuse continued in this fashion for four years until she graduated. Then she made her vow and left Riverside behind her forever.

*****

Mildred returned to Riverside, however. Despite her vow to leave her senseless past behind her, she returned to attend the funeral of her father. He had finally drunk himself to death, and she felt obligated to at least show up for the service. As soon as she stepped foot off the Greyhound bus, she felt an instant chill run down her spine. Suddenly, all the bizarre memories of a cruel home and an abusive teacher came rushing back to her battered mind. Mildred began to cry sorrowful tears down her rust-colored face.

A time in her life had come where she made the decision to change things. Mildred decided she was not going to be haunted by nightmares anymore. The therapy she received in upstate New York taught her she did not have to be the victim. She could now confront her fears and bring them to justice. The problem remains that Mildred still does not know how evil Mr. Cliff Brackstone really is. No one does.

Mildred walked quickly to the church to pay her respects, proud she had the nerve to come back to her town of hidden shame, but unaware of the predator she will face to revisit her past. "Eye for an eye" is how she envisioned her vengeful return. Though it is an outdated remedy for lingering shame, pure revenge is damn cheap and all Mildred can afford.

CHAPTER 6

School Is Out

JUST A COUPLE OF MINUTES after the last bell of the school day rang, Colette and Eileen talked happily by the lockers.

"What do you think we should do for the winter dance this year?" Colette asked Eileen, trying to pique her interest in a school event, though she knew Eileen could care less.

"I don't care, it's always the same old dumb thing. I go, no one asks me to dance, and then I scurry back home in about an hour to watch MTV," the plump young malcontent said with a frown.

Colette persisted though. "Oh, don't be silly, you should go. After all, you can hang out with me and Mat. I'll need some conversation which doesn't revolve around sports or sex."

The two giggled and proceeded down the hall, holding hands in a best friends' manner that only girls partake in.

"You want to come over tonight and watch a movie?" Colette suggested as they neared the exit doors of Riverside High.

Eileen thought a couple of moments about it, wondering if she would have enough time to deal with Mr. Brackstone and still make it over to Colette's at a suitable hour to watch the movie.

"Sure, I will come over. First, I have to take care of some after-school work, so I will meet you at your place later, okay?"

The two girls kissed on the cheeks softly and parted ways. Eileen made her way up to Mr. Brackstone's classroom. She stopped by her locker and retrieved everything she would need for homework then slowly rounded the corner to the science hall. She dragged her heavy feet up to the open doorway and peeked her plump head inside.

"Come in, sweetheart," whispered Mr. Brackstone to his shuffled little prize standing flumped over in his doorway. Mr. Brackstone could always sound really over-the-top at first with his victims. He developed his cheesy lines from years of watching poorly written soap operas in an inept attempt at understanding romance. Just the type of shit a lonely young girl like Eileen would fall for.

"I really love the way you look today, Eileen. That sweater really makes you look pretty. Have you done something new with your hair? It looks great!" Mr. Brackstone said invitingly to Eileen. She smiled cautiously, brushing her hair from her eyes. She entered the room at a slow pace.

"Close the door behind you, sweetheart," Mr. Brackstone said with an inviting yet spooky-looking grin which exposed his yellowish-brown teeth.

"Let's go back to our private little room. I have something I want to give you."

The back room of the science class looked more like a large closet filled with beakers, assorted rocks, and chemicals. If ever there was a place of torture and inhumanity on earth, this small eight-by-ten room was it. Countless rapes, murders, beatings, and depravities have smeared the walls, floors, and countertops of this shallow pit. The sick, twisted teacher saw it as his own personal macabre workshop, in which he was the only one making the rules and giving the grades.

Guiding Eileen into the hellish room with his arm around her shoulder, Mr. Brackstone revealed a stinking sweat mark under his armpit. Eileen noticed it and turned her head away from him just as they entered the room.

He smiled and said, "Surprise, Eileen!" producing a bundle of roses he bought for her at the local market that morning. A huge smile appeared on Eileen's fat face. She had never received roses before. She was so happy to see them she didn't notice Mr. Brackstone closing and locking the door behind her.

"Oh, Mr. Brackstone, they are so pretty. Thank you so much!"

"You know we have a very special relationship, don't you, sweetheart? And I want you to know you are the best thing in my life, Eileen. I truly mean that," Mr. Brackstone whispered in her ear as he put his hands around her, grabbing her oversize ass with his pale, disgusting hands.

Eileen tried to shy away. Mr. Brackstone quickly pressed his mouth to hers, placing his rancid-smelling tongue down her throat. Eileen submitted to the kiss, putting her hands behind Mr. Brackstone's head, feeling his greasy jet-black hair squirming between her fingers. The kiss soon graduated into Mr. Brackstone clumsily grabbing and tugging at Eileen's oversize breasts. He slowly removed her clothes, revealing the grotesquely overweight student underneath. She stood in front of him cold and naked. A quivering giant with flaps of mountainous fat folded over one another. Then Mr. Brackstone stripped down himself.

Eileen had never grown used to the sight of Mr. Brackstone naked. Even after three years of abuse, she still shuddered at the sight of his colorless, acne-infested body. His long, crooked penis stood erect in front of her. She knew the routine by now. Turning around to face the wall, Eileen felt Mr. Brackstone begin to suckle her fat-layered ass. In the shadowy reflection from the tin sheet next to her, she could see him taking advantage of her. Eileen tried to think of something else, the moment being too harsh for her to face.

Standing up quickly, Mr. Brackstone mounted Eileen from behind. Hunched over, sweat pouring down his forehead, Mr. Brackstone ripped into Eileen's innocence without a thought of compassion for his prey, pounding into her as though he were about to win a gold medal in the Olympics. The evil grin on his face could even be made out in the reflection from the tin sheet Eileen watched her aggressor in. It looked like a greyhound mating with a hippo. The sound of Eileen's wheezing and Mr. Brackstone's panting filled the tiny corners of the back room like harsh pornographic echoes in a canyon.

Eileen could hardly stand it much longer; her legs quivered from the stress she felt. Her heavy breaths and flushed face made her feel as though she would pass out any second. Mr. Brackstone pumped harder and faster. She moaned and heaved for air. His awkward, mis-shapen cock grew hard and sturdy within poor Eileen's walls. Then, all at once, with the howling of a sickly dog, Mr. Brackstone exploded inside her.

Eileen felt his slimy, warm semen running down the left side of her inner thigh, feeling humiliated and tired. Beads of sweat dripped profusely from her chubby face. Mr. Brackstone's reflection in the tin had become a mere shadow from the steam the two had produced. She thought it very strange that Mr. Brackstone did not pull out. He always did before. He had lectured her many times on how safe they have to be, to secure Mr. Brackstone's special relationship. A single tear ran down the side of her face as though she knew what was about to happen. Peering up to the tin again, she saw the shadow of a demon holding something in his hands. Mr. Brackstone's penis had not even exited her before he started beating her in the back of the head with an oversize lab microscope.

Mr. Brackstone ferociously smacked her two solid times over the back of the skull with the pointed edge of the weighty lab equipment. The first hit shattered the glass in the scope, making an ear-splitting sound on contact. The second split her skull like a fresh melon, sending a torrent of blood all over Mr. Brackstone's gangly naked body. This warm bloodbath gave him a massive surge of malicious vigor.

Eileen did not die instantly, to Mr. Brackstone's dismay. Rearing back with all her weight, she toppled the skinny naked demon over onto his back. Gushing blood uncontrollably from her head, she vehemently turned on her aggressor, jumping up and down on him again and again. Her flabby large ass cheeks pounded him in a fevered frenzy of fatty assault. Mr. Brackstone felt the crushing force of her two-hundred-pound body on his chest, cracking one rib with the first blow and then bruising his sternum with the next. She could have easily killed him if she had the energy to keep going, but the blood loss from her gaping head wound was making her woozy.

She knew she needed to get help fast. With Mr. Brackstone temporarily downed, she helplessly crawled for the door as fast as she could. Her blood-soaked hand toiled with the knob for a couple of seconds before she noticed, to her utter horror, it was locked. Upon rising to her feet, she heard Mr. Brackstone gathering himself behind her.

"No! No! No! You've been a very naughty little girl, Eileen!" Mr. Brackstone screamed while rising from his knees with an angry look on his repulsive, blood-soaked face. Eileen backed up against the door clumsily, crying.

"What am I going to do with you now?" Mr. Brackstone uttered while wiping some of her blood from his face. "I know, I'll teach you your final lesson, you little ingrate…how to die!"

Mr. Brackstone threw the bulky microscope at her head. The sharp corner of the shiny black object made an indent into her skull. Eileen slipped slowly down the door, leaving a blood trail from the back of her head. Her lifeless eyes rolled back in her head. She found herself gasping for air. With her final glance, she looked at the poor excuse for a man who just took her life. Disbelief filled her mind. Then, there was darkness.

CHAPTER 7

Forgive Me, Father

MILDRED PAUSED AT THE LARGE stone entrance of the red brick church. Her unattended hair grappled with her peculiar features on the wind's impractical command. She took a long deep breath and hesitantly entered the church at a solemn pace. Only a few vaguely familiar faces lined the pews. In front of the pulpit, she could see her father's withered face, sunk low in his casket. He was only in his early sixties, but the years of heavy drinking made his face look much older. Mildred found a seat in the front row and folded her hands in prayer preparation. A white-haired priest entered through the back doors and began to address the tiny group of mourners.

"Today we lay our brother Samuel J. Beron to rest. Samuel was taken from us by an evil addiction. I say this to all those who are here to witness: Know the beast in all of his forms. He will tempt you. He will drive you. He will hide in the shadows and ask you to sin. Whether it be at the bottom of a bottle or in the arms of lust, the beast most assuredly will test us all. Though we must remember, the beast is but a child in the shadow of our Lord. We can now pray that Sam has battled his demons long enough and is residing in heaven, at peace with his spirit. For none of us are lost to God. Let us remember what the Lord said in Revelations: *'Behold, I stand at the door, and knock: if any man hear my voice, and open the door, I will come in to him, and will sup with him, and he with me.'* You see, the Lord is just outside of our door. We know he is there asking to come into our lives. We need only let him in. In the name of the Father, the Son, and the Holy Ghost. Amen."

With the last prayers rendered, the organ bellowed a low, sullen tune. The few mourners that had come to pay regretful respects drifted out, leaving Mildred alone.

"Hello, Mildred," said Father Conner. He placed his sturdy hand on her slight shoulder to offer some comfort to her.

"I haven't seen you in a very long time, my child. I hope we have a chance to talk when you are ready."

Mildred cautiously looked up at the old priest. A solid stream of bitter tears began running down her face. She smiled, truly delighted to see the one person who had treated her decently in her turbulent adolescent years.

Father Conner was her sole comfort and solace in the stormy adolescent days she struggled through many years ago. Many times she had contemplated suicide; if Father Conner had not been there for her, she might have gone through with it. Always willing to listen or just give her a comforting embrace when she needed it the most, in a time when abuse was all Mildred knew, he showed her good still existed in the world.

"I knew he was going to die, and I didn't come to see him, not even once. Is that the most terrible thing you've ever heard?" Mildred whispered, weeping into her palms.

Standing her up, pulling her hands from her face, Father Conner smiled and offered his always-reliable consultation. "Sweet child, you still haven't learned to forgive yourself. It is not your fault he was a drunk. It is not your fault he is dead. You have to know that however sick your father was, he loved you. That is the only thing that matters. God has already forgiven you. Now it's time for you to forgive yourself."

Mildred began to blubber openly and pressed her face into the large Irish Catholic priest's soft chest. She felt a great release of emotion pouring from her soul. Having her father's death hanging over her head was not a load she could have possibly dealt with. Not with all the other emotional baggage she had strapped firmly around her back. To hear those words of comfort from her lone compatriot in life freed Mildred's soul and gave her strength.

The two old friends embraced for what seemed an eternity. Then, they sat down in the hard wooden pew to discuss the matter. Mildred calmed herself, then pulled a tissue from her pocket, and wiped her bloodshot eyes.

"I guess you're wondering what happened to me, huh?" Mildred said with a smirk.

"It had crossed my mind a time or two," replied the father with a loving grin.

"Well, after graduation, I had to get out. So I got on the first train I could find out of town, with no money, no plan, and no attachments to this miserable town. I haven't been back since. I went to New York for a while. Worked as a waitress. Eventually, I wound up in Virginia, taking some very inspirational courses. I got into studying some things that helped me realize there are a lot of peculiar issues I left unfinished in Riverside. It has taken a lot, but I'm back now to face my demons. No matter what happens now, I am stronger than I ever was. I have the confidence I once lacked."

By saying she was back to face her demons, the father figured she was talking about her abusive parents or the way the other children had treated her in school. He had no idea that one of those demons was actually a real one, in the flesh. What Mildred was about to tell Father Conner would bring a feeling to his body he hadn't felt for a very long time: rage.

In all the years Mildred had confided in Father Conner, they talked mostly about her abusive parents or the terrible things the other children at school said to her. Never once did she mention Mr. Brackstone. Though he knew she was having many difficulties because of the odd hand she had been dealt in life, Father Conner never could have imagined she was being raped by her own teacher.

Mildred looked at Father Conner and said, "Forgive me, Father, for I have sinned. When I was in high school, I was raped several dozen times by one of my teachers. I knew it was wrong. I was so ashamed of it that I just couldn't bring myself to tell you. I fear my silence has allowed this to go on with other girls. I have enabled this beast to go on hurting, raping, and God knows what else to innocent little children. I have come back to Riverside to bring him into the light, to bring justice to this town. I am no longer the weak little girl the kids called 'Rusty.' I need these sins to be rectified. This town needs release from this demon."

Reaching into her pocket, she pulled out an oblong black leather wallet and flipped it over to reveal a large picture ID of herself. Father Conner read the letters *FBI*, printed on one side in large blue letters.

"And now, old Rusty is just the girl for the job."

Shocked, Father Conner rose to his feet, with tears swelling up in his crystal-blue Irish eyes, his fists clenched tightly, and Father Conner howled, "I am so sorry I didn't help you! If I knew, I would never have let that happen to you, Mildred, you have to believe that. Please, tell me who this person is. We can finish this business together."

Mildred looked into Father Conner's old Irish face. She placed her hands on his cheeks and kissed his bloodshot forehead.

"No, Father, this is my demon. I must face this alone."

Mildred began to turn and leave.

"Mildred, wait. Take this." Conner slipped his black rosary beads over her head. "You are never alone in the fight against evil. If you need me, I am here for you always. I know I'm old, but you would be surprised at how well I can handle myself."

With a soft kiss on the old priest's hand, Mildred took one last look at Father Conner's weeping eyes and turned toward the doors. With a sense she now was truly on the side of good, she bravely headed out into the present to face her troubled past.

CHAPTER 8

The Cleanup

WASHING THE LAST DISGUSTING SPECKS of Eileen's already-dried blood from his grimy hands, Mr. Brackstone tossed a couple more tin cans into the recycling bin to cover the top of Eileen's split skull. Her lifeless eyes disappeared amid quick flashes of crumpled tin cans. It took Mr. Brackstone nearly twenty minutes just to hoist her obese body into the bin, then another thirty minutes to clean up the vast bloody mess he had made. Mr. Brackstone auspiciously peered into the bin while chucking a couple of bloody paper towels into it.

"Can't make an omelet without cracking a couple skulls."

Mr. Brackstone laughed like a hyena at his own sick joke. He wheeled the cart out of the back room and down the hall. He passed a group of meandering students on his way out. One of the class clowns even tossed a Coke can in the bin, screaming, "It's good! It's good!"

Mr. Brackstone ignored the mindless adolescents and continued his march through the long corridor. The recycling bin was on wheels but still posed a formidable weight for his slight muscles. A steady pounding built up in his chest at the possibility of getting caught. Yet Mr. Brackstone labored onward happily, avoiding notice. He neared the exit doors of the building, thinking he was home free. To his utter chagrin, Mr. Brackstone caught the attention of his school principal, Mr. Wong.

"Mr. Brackstone, I'm glad I caught you. We need to have a discussion about certain complaints I've been receiving about your grading this year."

Mr. Brackstone pulled the large bin behind him and faced his smug boss, then replied, "What kind of complaints are you receiving, sir?"

"Well, it seems that you are failing more than half of your class this year. That concerns me. We need to keep a status quo around here. We cannot afford to have half of your classes in summer school this year, can we, Mr. Brackstone?"

Mr. Brackstone grew somewhat angry but managed to hold himself back.

He mustered up his best ass-kissing smile and implored, "I understand that we have to push some students through, sir, but some of these kids don't even know what an element is, let alone what they are used for. I am teaching the same material from all of my previous years. These modern kids are just too interested in video games or MTV. They just don't do the work I assign for them."

"I understand all of that, Mr. Brackstone. Believe me, I don't want to ruffle your feathers. Just be aware we need to keep things running smoothly around here. Do we have an understanding?"

"Yes, Mr. Wong. I'm just doing my job."

"I understand that, Mr. Brackstone. You have to understand that I'm just doing my job as well. Hey, you know we pay our janitor's good money to take that stuff out. You don't have to do it."

Mr. Brackstone nervously looked down at the barrel behind him.

"I know that, Mr. Wong. I like to take a personal interest in conservation of our earth's precious resources."

"I wish there were more people like you, Mr. Brackstone. This world would be a much-cleaner place."

"I totally agree, sir."

Mr. Brackstone walked out the double doors toward the recycling dumpster and let out a great sigh of relief. A girlish giggle even hummed through his lips as he was thinking of Mr. Wong's ridiculous comment. He hurried over to the dumpster where he had already parked his old Ford pickup next to the recycling bin earlier in the day. His truck was hidden well by the large metal structure. It even blocked any possible views or vantage points from the school.

Mr. Brackstone struggled with Eileen's chubby body once again. It was not easy to lift two hundred pounds of dead, bloated weight, especially with a broken rib and bruised sternum.

He bent at the knees and pulled with all his might. The noisy rattling of tin cans filled the air. Mr. Brackstone removed as many of the cans as he could and plopped them into the dumpster. It took him several minutes to inch the obese form into the back of his pickup. He wrapped her in a blue weather tarp, very tightly, so not even the nosiest of student could tell what hidden secret Mr. Brackstone had in the back of his truck. He slammed the tailgate and scurried like a weasel to the wheel. Mr. Brackstone looked into his rearview and sighed.

He spoke to himself, "There is a lot of work to do, and not a lot of time to do it in. You did it again. You have proven your strength. You are a smart man, Mr. Brackstone."

Mr. Brackstone drove carefully through the parking lot. Each speed bump he hit sent Eileen's body flopping into the air a couple of inches. Luckily, no one noticed, and he headed down the road unscathed, proud of his latest massacre. He thought about what he needed to properly dispose of the body. Then realized he had to stop by the hardware store to get something sharp in order to hack into Eileen's oversize chest. He also needed a new hacksaw for her, having broken his last one sawing too brutally into a luckless victim.

Stan's Hardware Store is the only one in Riverside. Plus, it is conveniently located close to the waterfront. The rickety little shack that sells live bait and tackle turned out to be Mr. Brackstone's favorite store after his first couple of victims. He diligently entered the store knowing exactly what he needed. Finding both a sturdy hacksaw and a very fine-quality American-made tile knife, Mr. Brackstone had all his demented needs filled within five minutes. He approached the register, adamantly admiring his new toys.

Stan Morris patiently waited for Mr. Brackstone to come to the register. He was happy to see a customer on a weekday. Ever since the new discount home improvement store opened down the highway, business has been very slow.

"Hey, Mr. Brackstone. How are those rotten kids treating you over at school?"

Mr. Brackstone loathed small talk, especially with the country bumpkin types such as old Stan Morris.

"They are treating me just fine, Stan. You know I have a way with the kids. Even the ones who try to give me trouble."

Stan smiled, revealing a rock-bitten smile.

"Well, what can I do ya for? Looks like you got a dandy of a project going on. You know, if you need any help, I'm pretty good at fixing things up. And I work real cheap these days."

Holding back his amusement at the thought, Mr. Brackstone declined.

"No thank you, Stan. I like to get into these things all by myself. I develop sort of a special relationship with my projects. I'm sure you know what I mean."

"Whatever you say, Mr. Brackstone. Just make sure you don't bite off more than you can chew."

With the boring small talk over, Mr. Brackstone exited the store. He diligently drove down the road, determined to make it home without any more inconveniences. His truck stopped at one of the town's few red lights, and he looked into his rearview mirror. Right away, he noticed a bulging whitehead pimple on his throbbing neck. Mr. Brackstone quickly popped the oversize zit between his thumb and forefinger. The blood and puss burst out swiftly. He squeezed the remnants between his fingers and wiped it on his sweaty shirt.

Then, he looked back into the mirror to make sure he got all the puss out. His eyes caught movement in his rearview mirror. To his sheer disbelief, he noticed a familiar rust-colored face exiting the church directly behind his truck.

"What the fuck is old rust-face Mildred doing back here? I never expected to see you again."

Mr. Brackstone immediately noticed a difference in the way Mildred was carrying herself. She seemed confident, determined even. Thinking back, he remembered Mildred as a slumped-over, abused little girl. For the first time in his demonic career, Mr. Brackstone was scared. The feeling ran deep into his bones and enveloped his evil ambitions. None of the victims he let live ever came back to Riverside. Mr. Brackstone's brow dropped, and beads of sweat began pouring down his face.

"Fuck, shit, fuck, fuck, fuck!"

Mr. Brackstone beat on his steering wheel of the old pickup, throwing a world-class temper tantrum most three-year-old children would be proud of. Spit and snot covered his mouth. His normally pale face turned bright red.

Mr. Brackstone screamed through his mucus-covered mouth, "I will take care of you, you fucking bitch!"

Mr. Brackstone gripped the wet steering wheel until his hands turned red and his knuckles white from the pressure. He stared at Mildred with the devil's eyes, barely able to contain his rage. He was then startled; the resounding sound of a horn behind him brought his attention back to the light, which had changed. Peeling out around the corner, Mr. Brackstone rushed home to his garage. His deranged plans had just been escalated.

CHAPTER 9

Where Is She?

COLETTE LOOKED OUT OF HER second-story window for the tenth time at 8:00 p.m., helplessly wondering where her best friend was. She knew it was unlike Eileen to be late for anything they had planned. Most assuredly, Colette knew Eileen could never forget about the plans they made to spend time together. Deep in her heart, she realized something must be terribly wrong. Colette picked up the phone fretfully and called over to Eileen's house, naively hoping for the best.

Eileen's senile grandmother warily lurched over to the ringing phone. She had been raising Eileen since her disgraceful parents abandoned her many years ago. Raising an outcast child was well out of her decrepit reach, but she gave her a roof to sleep under, and in her opinion, that's all she could really do.

Finally reaching the phone through toil of crippling arthritis and poor hearing, the old woman blared into the receiver, "Who is it, and what do you want?"

"Hello, Grandma Pierce. Is Eileen home?"

Colette heard the strong echo of Grandma screaming upstairs for Eileen a couple of times.

"No, Eileen is not home right now. I always tell her to let me know when she is going to be late. But she never does. I'll tell you, kids these days don't listen to anybody. Who is this anyway?"

Colette held the phone out in front of her face in an attempt to protect her sensitive ears from the senile screaming voice on the other end of the line.

She screamed into the phone to make sure Grandma's ancient ears could pick up her voice, "This is Eileen's friend, Colette, from down the street. Can you ask her to call me when she gets home?"

A moment of silence passed from the other end of the line, followed by, "Sure thing, Suzette. I will tell her when she gets in. Good night."

Colette couldn't help but blurt out an immature giggle as she hung up the phone. Her amusement was immediately interrupted by a blank thought that buzzed through her mind for a couple of moments. An impasse of what step to take next blocked her usually sharp decision-making skills. It finally came to her all at once. She decided to call Mat and Tom for some much-needed help. When the two teenage malcontents arrived at her house, Colette was sick to her stomach over Eileen's absence.

"No one has heard from her since school let out," Colette impishly implied as Mat tried to comfort her in his large arms.

Mat openly suggested, "She could just be hung up somewhere. You never know what that girl is up to. Besides, it's not like she's a druggy or anything. Believe me, she is probably just hanging out somewhere with a guy she met."

"No, Mat, you're wrong. I know her, and she *never* breaks our plans. Just help me find her. I don't care if it is stupid. I want to know she is safe."

"All right, honey, you win. But I'm sure she is going to turn up and we will all feel a little stupid."

While Mat and Colette argued, Tom smacked his palm against the side of his head, trying to force out an idea. He then decided to check Eileen's house, and Mat suggested they look down by the park. After hours of fruitless searching, Eileen was still missing.

Colette suggested calling the police, but she was sidelined by Mat's hefty opinion, saying, "She has only been missing a couple hours, the local cops won't do anything for at least twenty-four hours. So let's just keep looking. She is bound to turn up somewhere."

The three students kept up the futile search for Eileen Pierce, not realizing she was already far beyond the point of rescue. Later that night, Colette reluctantly closed her bloodshot eyes and forced herself into a fitful slumber. Her thoughts grew indistinct, and her vision blurred, mixing together with subtle shades of red and black. She warped into a mindless dream.

Colette found herself holding hands with Eileen while walking down an iridescent hallway of Riverside High. Along the walls, there were banners for the local sports clubs in support of the upcoming homecoming celebration. Eileen gently squeezed her hand and emphatically smiled as they carelessly skipped down the long tiled floors. A rolling white mist grew in the distance and then began to slowly cover the ground. Colette vigorously squeezed Eileen's chubby hand. The plump digits resting in her palm seemed cold and clammy. A group of odd-looking girls all soaking wet and covered with mud ran past them at an unbelievable speed. The last girl was hideously deformed and uncaringly knocked Colette to the ground.

She could hear the cluster of oddities softly calling out to her friend, *"Come with us, Eileen, come join us. We are waiting for you…"*

As Colette gradually staggered to her feet, she witnessed Eileen following the group of drenched schoolgirls as they continuously called to her. The creepy crowd rounded the corner of the hallway and disappeared from sight. Eileen followed in tow, immediately rounding the corner of the hall.

Colette began yelling her name frantically. "Eileen! Wait for me, don't go down there!"

Colette gave chase. The lackluster hallway seemed to grow longer with each ensuing step. Everything slowed to a snail's pace. The scenery around Colette moved in slow motion. The heavy white mist on the ground circled around her body and danced in front of her eyes. Numbing deafness slipped into her mind at the discontent of her perusing spirit. As hard as Colette tried, she could not keep up with Eileen. Exhausted and utterly defeated, Colette gave in to the lonesome effects of her surroundings. With one sudden movement, she hit her knees whimpering.

"Eileen, come back. Don't go down there. Don't follow them…"

A second wind rushed into her youthful lungs. Defiantly rising to her feet, Colette gave open chase once again. This time, she found herself luckily gaining ground. The now cotton-white mist grew heavier around her body. Eileen stood perfectly still in the hall ahead of her. Plump and pail, she looked more like a ghost than her friend. Though they had disappeared into the cloudy vapor at the end of the hallway, Colette could still lightly hear the other girls calling out to Eileen in their sadistic siren song. Colette finally reached Eileen, gasping for air. She slumped over from exhaustion. The colorless fog had grown tall; it streamed down Eileen's face and around her plump body, hiding everything from sight but the two best friends.

"Why didn't you wait for me?" Colette said while still catching her breath.

"Shhhhhhhh. Did you hear that, Colette? He knows I'm here. Please, don't let him get me! I know he is here, waiting, watching. They want me to join them, Colette. I am so scared. I don't want to join them. Fear is the only thing I can feel. Please help me…"

Tears streamed down Eileen's portly face. Colette stood straight up and placed both of her hands firmly on Eileen's shivering shoulders. She started to ask who, but as her mouth opened, a vision of fear shot into her heart and froze her body. Two skinny, featureless hands crept from the depths of the haze. Unkempt long yellow nails foraged for a malicious landing. They wrapped around Eileen's face, digging into her soft flesh. Drops of fresh blood emerged under each vulgar nail. Eileen's eyes sharply widened. The devil's claws swiped her back into the hateful smog. Her voice could be heard screaming and crying Colette's name. A sinister laugh echoed in the impenetrable mist, and Colette stood alone in the hazy hallway.

An uncomfortable silence fell upon the scene, followed by several wet footsteps obviously moving in her direction. Through the mist, she could barely make out several forms heading in her direction.

She boldly spoke out, "What is happening? What do you want?"

The forms in the mist stopped, and a gargled voice replied, "You are next, Colette Jennings. You will soon be one of us. The best of us. We all want you to come join us. Join us in the deep…"

Colette woke up screaming incoherent babble. She floundered in a puddle of her own sweat. Crying like a young child, her mother rushed in and calmly hugged her.

"It's only a bad dream, sweetheart. It's just a dream."

Colette sank her head deep into her mother's chest and sobbed. She looked out her bedroom window into the night, wondering what in the world had happened to her friend.

CHAPTER 10

Down by the Delaware

MR. BRACKSTONE TOILED TO STRADDLE Eileen's bloated corpse. He ferociously cut at an awkward pace, splattering red decay carelessly over his hands. It took him nearly twenty minutes to saw through her massive chest bone with his shiny new hacksaw. Flakes of bone and crimson droplets of blood covered the grimy bed of Mr. Brackstone's pickup. His hands bore a close resemblance to that of a civil war field doctor. The stink of Eileen's dead body was enough to make his eyes water and his nose drip snot all over the front of his mouth. Her bowels had released on the ride home, covering the bed of the truck with rotting piss and shit. Mr. Brackstone did not have his garden hose set up to wash the rotting excrement from his tailgate. Instead, he struggled on through the unimaginable filth.

Finally, he successfully cut through the bone. Her chest split open, revealing the grotesque innards that Mr. Brackstone had grown accustomed to dealing with. Mr. Brackstone punctured both lungs then filled them with large stones he had collected the day before. He added a large helping of gravel and dirt into the remaining chest cavity to weigh her down. The mixture of coagulated blood and dirt-encrusted gravel produced a new smell of musty death.

Another large helping of snot poured across his thin lips. Unaffected, the monotonous death dealer sewed her chest back together with a crochet needle and bright-blue yarn. Mr. Brackstone sat back on his hands, admiring his devious work. Eileen's lifeless eyes stared at him as though she were still alive.

"Now, don't look at me like that, sweetheart. I had to take care of you. I saved you so much suffering and pain. Everybody always laughs at you and mocks you behind your back. Not me. I am your special man. I took care of it all, baby. Now go to sleep, I have other students to teach. They won't laugh at you anymore."

The lifeless corpse remained motionless, but Mr. Brackstone could hear Eileen's voice speaking out to him. *"I trusted you, Mr. Brackstone. How could you do this to me? We had something special."*

Mr. Brackstone jammed one of the needles into her throat. In a wild tone, he replied defiantly, "We didn't have anything special, you pathetic oaf. I used you. You were merely a pawn in my ultimate game. Now you are dead. Just like the rest of them. You meant nothing to me!"

Mr. Brackstone stood up and turned away from Eileen. He put his hands over his ears and curled his fingers in his black hair.

"Shut up, you stupid bitch! Stop talking to me. You are deformed and weak. You are dead. You can't hurt me anymore. Shut up!"

Mr. Brackstone hopped out of the bed of the pickup and grabbed some old soiled rags. He hurried back over to Eileen and stuffed the rags in her mouth. Then using the long needle from her throat, he continuously rammed the soiled rag deeper and deeper into the soft flesh at the back of her mouth.

"Shut up! Be silent. You are dead. You are dead, mother!"

Mr. Brackstone panted and slumped over Eileen's corpse. Crying for what seemed hours, oddly hung over his obese victim in a morbid embrace, he slowly regained his composure and closed her eyelids. He placed the weather tarp back over her body and hopped down from the truck.

Sneaking into his lonesome house, Mr. Brackstone walked wearily to his mantle of pictures. He looked at his bloody body in the mirror which was affixed to his dresser. Overwhelmed with a sense of accomplishment only experienced by the sickest of criminal minds, Mr. Brackstone opened the top drawer and pulled out a gold-framed picture of Eileen. Her chubby face looked pleasingly innocent. He placed her stout-faced picture among the ranks of his other victims.

With a sniveling grin and an evil chuckle, Mr. Brackstone uttered an unwelcome phrase. "Welcome home, Eileen. These are your sisters. I hope you like it here. They all do."

Without delay, he opened up the drawer again and pulled out an empty frame. Mr. Brackstone slipped a breathtaking picture of Colette Jennings into the open slot.

"It's time for you to learn your lesson now, popular girl."

Mr. Brackstone scurried off to the garage to finish his work. He secured Eileen's body quickly in his pickup and headed down the road toward the Delaware River. In Riverside, there is an abundance of hidden access points to the murky river. Most of the old loading docks for fishing boats and clam diggers have long been forgotten by the locals. Riverside's resident serial killer knows every one of these ports, however. He purposefully hunted for such places in his earlier teaching years.

Hundreds of small wooden plank docks riddle the banks of the river. Some hold single fishing boats, while others stand empty altogether. There are a couple of sailboat docks that hold multiple craft, but they fall farther down the river away from Mr. Brackstone's stomping grounds. All the docks are guarded well from view by tall waving swamp grass and large green maple trees. He uses them in sequence so as to not dump too many bodies in the same area. Mr. Brackstone's theory is that even if a body happened to float up, even if the cops drug the river, they would have a hard time finding the others.

The Delaware does most of the work for Mr. Brackstone. On some days, it is a very calm, placid river you can see the shoreline reflection in. On bad days, it is a raging river of undertows, rip-tides, and wild currents. The only swimmers the river gets are those with unnatural suicidal tendencies. So after preparing a body, Mr. Brackstone merely has to slip it in under the cover of night, and the cold river does the rest.

Pulling up slowly to the river, Mr. Brackstone slithered from his truck. Eileen's body was at least three hundred pounds by now, so

Mr. Brackstone backed the truck up on an incline. His pasty white face filled with blood as he tried with all his might to hoist Eileen's body into the river. Streams of sweat ran down his skeletal features. He tried time and again to no avail to force the oversize blob from his truck. Mr. Brackstone kicked, pounded, and stomped on Eileen's corpse.

Whimpering like a chastised child, Mr. Brackstone pleaded, "Get the fuck out of my truck! Get out, get out…get the fuck out!"

Finally, he fell to his knees in exhaustion.

"How the hell am I going to get this lard ass out of my truck?" he said to himself.

Peering to his right, he saw his sick-minded salvation. A small wooden fishing boat was roped off to one of the floating docks not even fifty yards from where Mr. Brackstone was toiling with his over-size load. Mr. Brackstone hustled over to the boat. He was in luck. He noticed right away it was a crank engine. Turning the engine over, he motored down the dark water to where the truck was parked. He tied some rope to the fishing boat then trudged over through the mud and tied the other end around Eileen's thick neck.

Hurrying back to the boat, Mr. Brackstone cranked the engine again and set out full throttle. Water shot off the line as the slack picked up. The small craft hummed forward and ripped Eileen's fat head right off her body.

"Oh shit!" Mr. Brackstone said as he spun the small vessel back around, Eileen's head following in tow.

He pulled the line in and grabbed the grotesque, severed head of his young victim. He picked it up gingerly; a large piece of her neck bone hung below the flapping flesh. Mr. Brackstone inspected the bone curiously.

Flipping it back upright, he dried off Eileen's mouth then kissed it, saying, "You just don't want to leave me, do you, sweetheart?"

The contemptuous monster tossed her head on the floor of the boat as if he were throwing down some old garbage. He then jumped out again. This time, he tied the rope around her large waist. Mr. Brackstone throttled the engine once again. The rope cascaded water and tightened. Eileen's body slid grudgingly out of the truck and splashed into the river, making a loud noise. Mr. Brackstone instinctively ducked down and peered around to check his perimeter.

He leisurely tugged Eileen's corpse toward the middle of the river for a couple of minutes and stopped the boat. Mr. Brackstone pulled as much rope in as he could, struggling against the weight of his victim and the pull of the undertow. When he grew tired and couldn't pull the rope in anymore, he cut it. The large, headless, ominous blob that was once Eileen Pierce floated for mere seconds but was soon sucked under the water, never to be seen again.

Mr. Brackstone took some leftover rope and tied it around Eileen's severed head along with a large piece of flat stone he grabbed off the shore. He reached back with all his strength and flung Eileen's lifeless expression into the Delaware. Her head flipped about in the air wildly, flinging dirt and blood over the water. It splashed into the cold depths and made an odd thumping sound. The head reemerged and floated like a horrible death marker on the river Styx.

Eventually, the undertow carelessly sucked all that was left of Eileen into the murky water. The student soul taker looked on, smiling and plotting. The deeds of evil men entrenched throughout his soul, and the future of evil deeds was hard at work in the dark reaches of a remorseless killer's mind.

CHAPTER 11

New Blood

COLETTE WORKED AT IT BUT could hardly concentrate through her boring morning classes. Her habitual concern over Eileen's whereabouts was seen by her friends as a bit premature. Eileen was prone to bouts of depression. Sometimes, she would miss days of school at a time. So her absence was not seen as a huge event at school. However, Colette knew something was wrong. She just had to figure out what happened to her friend. Tormented thoughts about the worst possible scenarios were killing Colette inside. So she decided to snoop around school and see what she could find.

Colette was not without grand high school resources. In the hierarchy of things, she sat on top of the throne and ruled above all. She ordered Tom to jimmy open Eileen's locker so she could go through her stuff. Tom really didn't want to do it, but Colette's pretty smile and bossy manner were too much to combat over the issue. Inside the locker, they found the usual high school girl junk: a couple of boy-band pictures, various class-related books, a box of Hostess Twinkies, which where Eileen's personal favorite. Nothing really stood out except one little typed note folded up at the bottom of her locker that read:

> *You look very pretty today, sweetie. Make sure you are careful. We don't want anyone finding out about our special relationship. I know things are*

hard now, but they will get better soon. If you need anything, I am here for you. Just remember to keep our secret.

The note was unsigned, but it brought a sense of shock to the two snoops.

"How could Eileen have a boyfriend?"

Colette actually began to get pissed over the issue. After all the times she had tried to set Eileen up and failed, she never once told her about this boy.

Tom touched her shoulder and said, "See, Colette, she is probably off with this guy somewhere, taking care of a little BSB."

"What is BSB, Tom?"

Tom massaged her shoulder and said in cheesy teenage voice, "You know, BSB: back seat business."

"Oh, that is really mature, Tom. Why do all of you guys have to think with your cocks?"

Tom looked puzzled then replied, "Because that's where God put our brains, Colette."

"Well, guess what, Tom, you have a really small 'brain' if that's what you really think."

Colette pushed past Tom and stuffed the note in her pocket, determined to confront Eileen with it as soon as she found her. Tom convinced her there was nothing else they could find. They wandered down the hallway to class, both wondering who Eileen's secret lover was. As the two malcontents entered science class, Mat quickly joined them.

"Any luck, Nancy Drew?" Mat said jokingly. Colette whacked him in the head with her purse.

"You're such a jerk sometimes, Mat. You don't even care about my feelings. Why don't you just find someone else to sit with today?"

Colette pushed past him and sat at the far table.

"Jeez, what did I do?" Mat said as Tom walked by.

"You thought too much with your 'brain,'" Tom snickered as he took his seat.

"Take your seat, class," a bellowing voice came from the hallway. The class quickly sat down. Sniveling under his breath, Riverside's resident science teacher Mr. Brackstone entered the class looking awfully ragged and insipid. His jet-black hair slicked back in such a careless manner it revealed the pasty white bald spot in the back of his skull. Kmart Blue Light Special dress shirt was only half tucked. His tie hung so crooked it touched his purple pocket protector over his left breast. By the looks of it, Mr. Brackstone had a seriously rough evening.

"Too many beers last night, Mr. Brackstone?" Mat said under his breath. The rest of the class laughed and giggled.

"That's very funny, wise guy. How would you like to tell that to the principal?" Mr. Brackstone uttered in his usual insecure tone.

The class hushed as he handed out the lab assignment. Mr. Brackstone made his way to the back of the room where Mat was sitting and confronted the popular jock jokester.

"So, Mr. Pistone, do you think it's funny to make fun of my appearance?"

Mat put his face in his chest, holding back his laughter, and responded, "Gee, I'm sorry, Mr. Brackstone. It will never happen again, I promise. Oh, please don't call my parents! It would just crush them."

The class giggled again, and Colette motioned for Mat to stop. His youthful angst was approaching full-out disrespect. Mr. Brackstone paused for a moment until the class hushed once again.

"So you think everything is a joke. Okay, well, how is this for a joke… The entire class has to turn in a five-page paper on Sir Isaac Newton and his laws by the end of the week, or you all will fail this semester."

Loud groans and muffled curse words echoed throughout the class. Mat stared hard at Mr. Brackstone in defiance. He balled his fist up and held back the urge to let one fly.

"Now, Mr. Pistone, do you have any other jokes you would like to share with the class?"

Mat bit his bottom lip so hard he could taste his own blood. Voices from the crowded classroom urged him to keep his mouth shut. Colette sternly looked at him, demanding silence without even speaking a word. Mat sank his head down and tried to calm his raging testosterone.

"We are waiting, Mat. Everyone here wants to see how daring you are. Come on now. You're not going to just let me push you around like that, are you? Do you have another joke or not?"

"No, sir," Mat responded from the corner of his mouth.

Mr. Brackstone leaned in close to Mat's face and whispered, with his thin lips mere inches from Mat's earlobe, "Good. Now that paper better be first-rate, or it could mean an early end to your athletic season. *Now* who's laughing, jock?"

Mr. Brackstone leisurely walked to his desk and took his seat and began peering through his tinted glasses at Colette Jennings, unquestionably the loveliest girl he had ever seen in any of his classes at Riverside High. Her long, onyx-black hair enticed him daily, resting gently on her subtle shoulders. Strong, defined features resembled a young Brooke Shields without the bulky, overgrown eyebrows. Soft eyelashes batted over the lightest baby-blue eyes Mr. Brackstone had ever seen. Her blouse was slightly opened, which gave Mr. Brackstone a straight angle at her breasts, milky white and perky, even without a bra. He could even catch the slightest hint of her pink nipple brushing up against the white cotton interior of the blouse.

Small droplets of perspiration began to drip down Mr. Brackstone's greasy black hair. He could feel his skinny, shriveled penis begin to fill with blood. Colette brandished a sleek pair of cut-off blue jean shorts, the kind all the young girls on MTV flaunt to impress millions of ogling onlookers. Her outfit alone was enough to drive Mr. Brackstone to the edge of explosion. Long muscular legs glistened in the fluorescent lights of the science room, inviting Mr. Brackstone's perverted eye-raping while infusing his demented spirit with ghoulish lust. The frayed edges of her shorts gave an intimate peek at the bottom of her ass, slipping out to entice any onlooker. Even her sandals exposed a set of dainty, pretty feet. Mr. Brackstone peeped and imagined his way into a full-fledged raging hard-on.

He tucked his body under the desk so as to not expose his excitement and then wiped his brow with his clammy palms. He began to stroke his cock under the desk with his free hand, sadistically gazing at Colette, immersed in his self-indulgence. Suddenly, the bell rang to end the period. Mr. Brackstone, still in full arousal, was startled. The students began flocking to his desk with their lab reports. They dropped them one by one onto the green table cover, mere inches above his hidden dirty deed. Slumping over in an obvious nature, Mr. Brackstone hid his arousal successfully from the students.

As the last of the students poured out, he frantically sat back in his chair, satisfied in his success. Just then, Colette Jennings stuck her pretty head back into the classroom. Mr. Brackstone quickly hunched over his desk again.

"Mr. Brackstone, do you know where Eileen is?"

The question caught Mr. Brackstone off guard. Why would the most popular girl in school care about that blob of shit?

"No, Colette, I don't. Why do you ask?"

Colette bounced into the room and leaned over Mr. Brackstone's desk, fully exposing her ample cleavage to his prowling eyes.

"Well, we were gonna watch a movie last night, and she never showed up. I know she said she had some work to do after school, so I figured she might have come in here for extra help. Her grandmother hasn't seen her, and I am starting to get worried."

Mr. Brackstone saw Colette's complete concern. The revelation that Colette cared for her fallen friend revealed the sneaky pervert's opportunity of a lifetime. His brow lifted; he regained his confidence and made a generous offer.

"Well, if she is still missing after school, I will be happy to help you look for her, Colette," Mr. Brackstone said with a concerned look on his face.

"That would be great, Mr. Brackstone. Everyone else thinks I am overreacting. I will come by after school, okay? See, I knew you were a good guy behind all that tough talk."

Colette skipped out of the classroom happily, not knowing she had just made a date with the devil. With the stage set, Mr. Brackstone sat back in his seat and reached for his pathetic manhood again. In mere seconds of furious stroking, he reached climax. Mr. Brackstone hunched over his mess and reveled in his own devious planning. *How could this have worked out so perfect?* he thought to himself. Mr. Brackstone stewed in his glory, pondering the many different atrocities he could perform on Colette. The very thought of deflowering her gave Mr. Brackstone spiteful motivation. The kind of drive inspired by years of torture, rape, and murder. The kind of viciousness only a demented killer can bask in.

CHAPTER 12

Papers to the Past

MILDRED PULLED HER UNCOMFORTABLE METAL seat close to the buzzing computer screen. Squinting her weary eyes, she mindlessly looked through the missing-children section of the Riverside Police Department archives. Mildred found countless cases of abused children who have gone missing. Though there could have been any number of reasons for a kid to have gone missing, nine times out of ten, it was a result of abuse, in one form or another.

The pages all blended together into a green computer haze. Hundreds of girls, millions of stats; it could take weeks to find what she needed.

She thought deeply, and then asked herself, "What is the connecting factor to all of Mr. Cliff Brackstone's victims? There must be a piece of the puzzle that I am missing…"

After several more hours of searching, she still came up flat. Blazing eyes hardly able to see the computer screen caused pain reflexes to shoot off in her brain, sending nervous twitches through her tired eyes. The inflexible back of the chair dug into the small of her back like a dull knife making her feel like two cinder blocks were resting firmly on her shoulders, pushing her to the brink of exhaustion. Then, a moment of clarity came upon Mildred like a thief in the night. The concept was so effortless, yet she overlooked it so many times.

The one connecting factor that linked her with the other victims Mr. Brackstone had molested now became painfully obvious.

"Nothing!" she yelled out loud through her drowsy voice.

Nothing. They are the girls at the high school that nobody missed, including, and most of all, their own family members. The Nothings.

"The Nothing Girls."

Mildred stumbled upon her curious attachment with the others. The reason she was chosen for this morbid mission. Excommunication from the social fabric of high school made her and all the other girls the perfect victims for Mr. Brackstone, the girls no one ever cared about or would ever miss.

Quickly, Mildred began to look up the girls who were reported missing by resources other than their parents during Mr. Brackstone's teaching tenor. She eliminated the popular girls and the drug addicts. The list of girls that filed out was one of virtual nobodies, girls who became faded memories within days. Some of the missing-person sheets didn't even have contact numbers in case they ever turned up. Pictures from the reports revealed frumpy, ugly, and physically challenged girls. These are the names and faces Mildred has been looking for all her life, her sisters of mediocrity, her sorority of solitude. Mildred found her family on the rap sheets. Her mission became clear: to find out what became of Mr. Brackstone's Nothing Girls.

"How many of these girls have turned up dead?" she asked herself out loud.

The next step took Mildred to the paper archives. She panned through thousands of obituaries. No luck in any case. Mildred could not believe these girls could just vanish off the face of the earth. The sheer terror Mildred felt imagining a mass grave site underneath Mr. Brackstone's house sent shivers down her spine. She hoped and prayed there might be a clue to what happened to the Nothing Girls. In the end, after countless hours of mind bruising paperwork, she was left with only the list and a hunch.

Mildred thought back to her psychological profiling classes at the academy. She began to develop a pattern on Mr. Brackstone's thought process. Putting herself in his shoes, she considered what Mr. Brackstone might do with the girls if they ever became a problem.

"Mr. Brackstone is smart, there is no question about that. The fact is, almost all serial killers test out well above normal intelligence levels. Some are even genius status."

Knowing what she did about Mr. Brackstone gave her a tremendous advantage. Mildred devised that Mr. Brackstone may be smart, but he always liked to keep things simple. Even though it brought back painful memories, Mildred thought back to when Mr. Brackstone raped her. Mildred hesitantly remembered the slow-paced sex act, always in the same position, never breaking stride. Mr. Brackstone made the entire experience simple to perform, simple to cover up, and simple to start over. Though he made minor efforts at comforting, Mr. Brackstone always kept his distance.

At the time it was happening, she thought Mr. Brackstone was just unaffectionate. But now, she realized he was making it easy to eliminate a victim if need be. By now, Mildred had come to the startling end of her paper search—a list of names, no leads to where they might be, or what Mr. Brackstone had done with them—unaware that just a few blocks away, in the harsh Delaware River, the young victims she was eternally related to in pain lay waiting to be avenged.

CHAPTER 13

Snooping

FATHER CONNER WAS ALWAYS A man of action. When the town flooded, he always rushed to be the first filling sandbags to help. When the Little League teams needed a coach, he was the first to volunteer, even if he never played the sport. Mildred should have known he was not going to sit on his ass while there was a wolf among his flock of sheep. Father Conner had the blessing of an incredible memory.

It was only a matter of time before his number one suspect was unveiled to be Mr. Cliff Brackstone. During his talks with Mildred many years ago, she had mentioned him as a man who was helping her out with stuff at school. Father Conner wasn't sure, but there was only one way for the old priest to find out, and that was going to require some snooping.

Just outside Mr. Brackstone's dilapidated dwelling, Father Conner peered through a side window. Removing caked-on dust with his shirtsleeve, he saw a dresser with some frames on it, but he couldn't make out any faces. He noticed right away the room was in disarray along with the rest of the house. Creeping around back, the old priest forced the back door opened and entered the foul-smelling home. The walls were stained yellow and brown from years of neglect and water damage.

A rat scurried across his feet and made the elderly man jump back against the kitchen counter. Father Conner placed his hand on the countertop to stop himself from slipping. He felt something wet and sticky tangling with his fingers. Looking over his shoulder, the old priest noticed he had just put his hand into a mush of old fruit covered with maggots. The crouched white larva crawled all over Conner's fingers, searching for an opened wound to infest. He quickly pulled his hand from the goo and ran over to the sink. In a rush, he turned the faucet on and washed his hands. Looking down, he noticed a hacksaw and a tile knife covered in what seemed to be human blood. The mere sight of these items made Father Conner nauseated. His worst fears had been realized, and the strong sense of faith he had always felt seemed to wither in the moment. He had to fight back the vomit building up in his throat. Upon further inspection, Conner found bits of bone and skin on the outskirts of the jagged blades of the hacksaw. He realized he was sitting in the middle of a modern-day torture chamber.

Conner thought to call 911 for a moment, but his curiosity got the best of him. He forced his snooping nose into the next room. The filth that permeated inside Mr. Brackstone's house was disgusting. Conner barely took a step without feeling something squish under his feet. The floor was littered with old newspapers, magazines, and fast-food bags. The dust-covered television looked as though it hadn't been turned on in years. Spiderwebs lined every doorway plagued with helpless flies. The smell was so rancid Conner had to put a hanky over his nose just to maintain a clear airway.

On the wall hung a lone picture of John Merrick, his disgusting form fully exposed, the grotesque nature of his existence in plain sight. This said so much to the old priest about Mr. Brackstone's ego. Though Mr. Brackstone is not as physically repulsive as the Elephant Man, he must relate to his plight. An outcast of society, made fun of by his peers. This could drive a man to do horrible things.

"What have you done?" whispered the old priest as he peered at the picture.

The rest of the house was just as disgusting as the kitchen and living room. As Conner walked into the master bedroom, he grabbed at his own heart. He saw all the pictures of the girls, framed in gold on Mr. Brackstone's dresser. He picked up the picture of Mildred, who was looking away from the camera, hiding her birthmark. A sympathetic tear came to the old man's weathered face. Looking at the rest of the pictures, he grew irate. All the girls societal rejects, all young, innocent, and now, probably most of them dead.

Conner tried as hard as he could to not throw up, though it wouldn't make much difference in this place. Suddenly, something caught Conner's eye. There on the end of the table, a picture different from the others. At first, he thought it was just one of those generic model pictures the companies put in as fillers, but upon closer inspection, he found out, to his dismay, it was Colette Jennings. Colette was a devoted member of his flock at the church along with her family. Conner's jaw dropped. He now knows who Mr. Brackstone is going after next.

He thought she may be in the house at this very minute. Conner left the room and searched the rest of the house frantically for any clues or remains he could use to incriminate Mr. Brackstone. On his way up the stairs, Conner could hear soft music coming from the attic space. The door at the top was locked, and a faint light glared from beneath the door. He knocked twice and then pounded on the door, but he received no response. The crafty old priest took out his Swiss Army knife and popped the hinges off the door, slamming it open, expecting to find Colette or perhaps even another girl.

Instead, the priest found something he had only seen in horror movies: an altar with the sign of the beast painted against the wall. The faint music he heard was being played on a repeating compact disc player in the corner of the room. When he turned it up to hear the words, he realized it wasn't actually music at all. It was the horrific screams of young girls, continually looped and played over and over again. The old priest turned away from the compact disc player and bumped against the altar. He noticed a book on top of the altar seemingly coved in blood. Turning the first page, he read the title of this sick journal:

The Life and Times of a Monster
By Mr. Cliff Brackstone

Flipping through the book, Conner noticed bits of hair and blood mixed in with the ramblings of a madman. Most of the book was about the sick details of rape and torture that drove this sick demon to do his unspeakable deeds to innocent youth. Some of it talked about the relationship he had with his parents and how he wished he was never born.

One particular paragraph took the old priest by surprise when he came across his own name. Mr. Brackstone had mentioned how the only force for good in the whole town was a weak and mindless priest who could not even tend to his own flock. This brought Father Conner to the brink of rage. He shook his old fists in defiance at what he had just read. Thinking he now had the perfect evidence to take down this madman, Father Conner dug his nails beneath the setting of the book to remove it from its satanic altar. As he pulled the book from its cheap table framing, he heard a zipping sound. Looking beneath the book, he noticed a string was attached to the bottom of the binding. Subsequently from under the altar, Father Conner heard a *whoosh* then felt an uncomfortable crunch. Looking down gradually, the old priest saw his legs impaled by a two-by-four covered with rusty nails and razor blades.

The old priest began to bleed from multiple gaping wounds. The pain, so unbearable he couldn't even muster enough energy for a scream. Reaching down, he tried to pull the crude booby trap from his legs, but he couldn't manage to free himself. He noticed something written on the back of the impaled board: *"You are fucked! The nails are poison. I hope you die in utter pain!"*

Such terror struck Conner's heart he began to weep openly, not for his own life, which was about to end, but for the lives of all the girls he could not avenge. He began to feel a burning in his wounds; it must be the poison taking effect. Conner took the cross from around his neck and began to administer the last rites to himself. The burning turned into a blaze, crawling its way up Conner's legs and into his chest. His muscles felt tight around his failing heart. It became hard to breathe. He felt a trickle of blood begin to run down his nose; the burning moved all the way up to his neck. With his last words, Conner prayed to God to avenge the many victims of this living devil.

"Lord, please come to the aid of this humble town. Watch over these people. Protect them from Mr. Cliff Brackstone. Show this devil your power and bring him to justice."

With his last amen, the old priest gasped for his last breath of air. Both of his eyes swelled with blood. A mixture of clear fluid and crimson-red blood burst out of the sockets, splattering against the attic walls. His tongue grew so large his natural instinct to breathe forced him to bite half of it off. The bloody nub in his mouth spewed blood down his chin. The severed portion of his tongue still flipped around, fighting for life on the attic floor. Without warning, his lungs collapsed. Blood came pouring out of his mouth as if from an opened faucet. His lifeless body lay before the satanic altar in the attic of the beast. A frozen look of utter surprise was all that remained on his pail and bloody face. With the satanic screams of helpless victims playing in the background, Father Conner went to meet his Maker.

Chapter 14

The Big Prize

THE LAST BELL OF THE school day rang out like the beginning of a prize fight had just started. Mr. Brackstone worked at his desk, collecting papers from his last-period class as the students filed out into the hallway. Eagerly anticipating Colette's arrival, Mr. Brackstone's black heart raced so rapidly he could barely contain his sick aggressions. Thoughts of torture and rape poured through his mind as he sat knock-kneed, pondering his future deeds. The plan was simple, the same as it always has been.

Mr. Brackstone spoke to himself in a low whisper, "Play weak, act like the lowly science teacher all the children mock and ridicule until the right moment. Then, strike with no mercy."

"Hey, Mr. Brackstone, are you ready to help me find Eileen yet?" asked Colette as she floated into the small cold science lab.

"Well, let me get a couple of things in order here, and then you will have my full and undivided attention on the matter of hunting down your missing friend, okay?" Mr. Brackstone said in his best wimpy science teacher voice.

He delicately gathered his things. Mr. Brackstone could not believe his luck. She had walked right into his hands. With his back turned to her, Mr. Brackstone struck an evil expression that could have scared a Nazi. He mashed some lab papers into his cheap briefcase. Completely excited, he dropped a rubber band full of number 2 pencils which scattered onto the floor.

"Oh shit," Mr. Brackstone blurted out as he began to pick up the strewn-about pencils.

Colette dropped to her knees to help the dorky little man out. Her skinny long legs lingered up her shorts, and a large portion of her ass sneaked out the side, as usual. Mr. Brackstone stopped dead in his tracks and stared like a deer in headlights at her perfect form. He felt the blood rush away from his head and into his crotch again. The worst thing he could do now was get aroused. So he closed his eyes and tried to think of something else. Panic dripped down Mr. Brackstone's face. He opened his eyes and caught a glimpse of Colette's pink G-string sneaking down the crack of her ass.

This is too much to take, Mr. Brackstone thought to himself. Now in full raging hard-on form, there was only one sure escape. Mr. Brackstone grabbed for his briefcase and stood up quickly. He strategically placed the briefcase in front of his boner so as not to be detected. At that moment, Colette rose to her feet and placed the remaining pencils inside the case Mr. Brackstone was holding, only inches from his premature excitement.

"Well, now that we have all the pencils taken care of, can we get started, Mr. Brackstone?" Colette said through a sarcastic smile.

Mr. Brackstone sneered. "Absolutely, Colette, let's go find your friend."

Rounding the last corridor of the hallway to the parking lot, Mr. Brackstone's imagination was taking full control of the situation. He could think of nothing but the pretty young girl walking so eagerly beside him as he openly led her out to his truck. He opened the door for her, and she jumped into the front seat, needing no encouragement whatsoever. Mr. Brackstone started his pickup and slowly pulled out of the parking lot.

While fixing his greasy black hair in his rearview mirror, Mr. Brackstone asked, "Where would you like to start looking for your friend, Ms. Jennings?"

As the truck pulled out of the lot, Colette began to make suggestions of where they should start to look for her friend. Mr. Brackstone paid absolutely no attention to the words coming out of the young girl's mouth. He was becoming the creature he had to be in order to pull this off. All emotion escaped Mr. Brackstone's being. His face and arms became as pale as a ghost, and the right side of his lip rose up to reveal a yellow-toothed evil grin.

He began talking under his breath to himself in a sluggish, psychotic tone. "You think you're so perfect, you think you're so sweet."

Mr. Brackstone pulled off the road quickly into an old water runoff ditch hidden from the street by two hills. And the moment he slammed the car into park, he pounced on Colette with the awkward quickness of a striking snake. Colette was caught off guard but tried to struggle free. She was pinned against the door. The ether rag Mr. Brackstone had hidden under his seat in a ziplock back was soaked and ready to go. He slammed the rag against her mouth, and after a few seconds of struggle and one or two good kicks to Mr. Brackstone's stomach, Colette slipped into a deep sleep. Her beautiful, limp body slumped in the seat next to Mr. Brackstone as he positioned her out of sight to any onlookers.

Mr. Brackstone wrapped her wrists and ankles in duct tape and stuffed a dirty cloth in her mouth. Just looking at her unconscious body made his devilish impulses proud. He smiled from ear to ear, looking at what he had just accomplished.

"You're all mine now, sweetheart, and soon people will start to notice me for the true genius I am."

Turning his truck around quickly, he headed back to his house. There were so many things to pick up and such little time to do it. As he entered his driveway, he immediately noticed the back door was hanging wide open. Mr. Brackstone hurried inside to see what was going on, leaving the still-unconscious Colette behind in the truck. It only took a couple of seconds before he found the old dead priest, now covered with flies and smelling of human waste.

"So, old man, you finally figured it out. Well, hopefully, you learned a good lesson about staying out of other people's things," Mr. Brackstone said as he picked up Father Conner's head to inspect the effects of the poison.

A crimson stream of blood poured from Father Conner's mouth, and his body slumped flat on the attic floor. Mr. Brackstone stood over the body in triumph. He had never felt so proud of his intellect. Not only had he stolen the town's most adored princess; he also took out his only adversary. The emotionless monster proceeded to unzip his pants and urinate on the old man's corpse. The mixture of fresh piss and the smell of death were enough to make even the most strong-willed of men puke, but Mr. Brackstone reveled in it. This was his moment of victory, and he was going to take full advantage of the situation.

After shaking off the last few drops, Mr. Brackstone gathered up his necessary things: all his torture tools, his book, and his pictures from downstairs.

"Now I am ready to embark on my most daring campaign to date: the utter destruction of Colette Jennings."

CHAPTER 15

The Clock Tower

GROGGY, DAZED, AND CONFUSED, COLETTE Jennings finally returned to the conscious world. The first thing she noticed was her feet and hands individually bound to the wall. The knots were not tight, but they were very strong. With the first few attempts at biting at them, she realized it to be a futile effort. A repetitive clanging of gears and chains could be heard not too far away. Her head was still very light, yet she managed to get to her feet.

Colette found herself in a dusty small room that was only as big as her bedroom at home. There was a bed in the corner, and several roaches ran underneath it at the sound of Colette's awakening. A small dresser and table completed the furnishing of the room, and the only thing she could see, as far as an exit, was a trapdoor in the far-left corner of the room, well out of her bound reach. The reality of the situation hit Colette like a mountain of bricks.

I have been kidnapped by my science teacher. A million questions then ran through her head.

Is he going to kill me? Is he going to rape me? What does any of this have to do with Eileen?

Unfortunately for Colette, all these questions would be answered very soon. As she pondered on how bad of a situation she was really in, hearty tears flowed from the young girl's eyes. Her whole life, she had been guarded and protected against this sort of thing. Her parents always told her to watch her back and be wary of strange people.

An overly caring nature and good-hearted ways placed her into this mess in which there seemed to be no way out.

The hopelessness of it all broke Colette down to a sob. She cried for her parents at first, then to God while tugging desperately at her bonds. She was trapped in the dusty attic, ridiculously dressed in her cutoff shorts and skimpy top. Colette felt, for the first time in her life, what it was like to be truly alone. It was cold and dirty in the little room. Her heart seemed to beat out of her chest. All the tears in the world were not going to save her. She continued to cry in a hidden hope that someone might come to her aide. The thought of escape was already floating around her mind. She was searching for anything she could use to cut herself free. There was nothing. Enraged, Colette kicked the firm plaster wall, but that did not help either. The thick structure was made from poured concrete and covered with several layers of thick plaster.

As harsh as it was to face, Colette truly realized she was stuck. Delicately gathering herself up in a defensive ball, she hopelessly stared at the lingering trapdoor, knowing that soon Mr. Brackstone would come to visit, revealing the true depth of the moment. Colette will look the devil in the eyes and understand her fate.

Unexpectedly at that moment, the attic door crept upward. The insipidly scrawny figure of Mr. Cliff Brackstone unhurriedly emerged from the depths of the trapdoor. He still smelled of death from the house, and Colette had to hold her nose so as not to vomit. Mr. Brackstone entered the room without saying a word. He carefully placed his things on the bed and began to inspect them. Colette remained quiet, frozen with fear. Heavy breathing was the only sound that could be heard in the cold room. She curled back up into a ball and peered at Mr. Brackstone over her knees. He was slowly wiping off and arranging his golden-framed pictures by the weathered cot. It seemed odd to Colette he had not even noticed her yet, as if he didn't even see her in the room.

Then she thought, *Maybe I'll be okay. Maybe he just wants money.*

She spoke out to Mr. Brackstone in a submissive voice, "Mr. Brackstone, what are you going to do with me?"

Mr. Brackstone froze; his slight frame turned in slow motion to face Colette. He looked at her with the coldest gaze she had ever seen in her life. Then, his wicked nature took control. Like a starved cat on a cornered mouse, he pounced on her once again. Mr. Brackstone grabbed her face with one hand pressing her cheeks together, attempting to force his tongue down her throat. With the other hand, he quickly probed her young chest and firm stomach. Colette noticed right away she was considerably stronger than Mr. Brackstone. With one solid shove, she sent the slight man across the room crashing into the soiled cot and knocking over one of the pictures, which crashed to the floor and shattered the glass frame.

Mr. Brackstone sprang up and pounced again, this time landing on top of Colette's head. He forced it down between her legs, pinning her uncomfortably to the rigid wooden floorboards. He plunged his gnarly yellow teeth into the back of her neck and clamped down, drawing blood instantaneously. Colette was stricken with pain. She tensed up her back and reared against her aggressor. Now, she had a clear shot at Mr. Brackstone's groin. With all the strength she had, Colette clamped down on Mr. Brackstone's gangly balls, digging her nails into the soft sensitive skin of his scrotum. Mr. Brackstone was stunned by how painful her grip was. The traumatized perpetrator sprang to his feet with the little hellcat holding on for dear life. He screamed in pain, subsequently punching Colette harshly across the bridge of the nose. Colette's head bounced off the wall behind her, and blood began to gush out of her nose and down her pretty face. Unsuccessful, Mr. Brackstone pulled away, scurried into the corner of the room, leaving small shreds of his ball sack under Colette's well-manicured nails, out of her reach. The diminutive scavenger agonized in pain as his wounded balls began to swell immediately.

Colette gathered herself after a couple of seconds and stood up.

"Come on, you sick son of a bitch! Get your little ass back over here, and I'll *rip them off* this time!"

Mr. Brackstone safeguarded himself in the corner. He hurriedly stood up, staying out of her range.

"Okay, okay. You win for now, Colette. You are much stronger than I had anticipated. But…let's try a little science experiment.

We'll just wait a couple of days. Deprive you of all food or water. Give you no access to a toilet. My theory is, you won't be as strong after time passes. And then when you're weak, when you can hardly move, when this place is covered in your urine and shit, I'm going to come for you, Colette. I'm going to rape you over and over again. Until you can't remember how many times it's been. Then I'm going to cut your perfect petite heart out and mail it to your fucking parents!"

CHAPTER *16*

Boyhood Dreams

THE BATTERED MASTICATOR SORROWFULLY SAT on the soiled cot, agonizing in testicular pain. His tormented testicles throbbed as if his heart had moved south from his chest directly into his swollen crotch. Each entrenched puncture mark extenuated the already-unbearable pain, forcing the rejected aggressor into the dark recesses of his demented mind. He closed his eyes and faded into a sleeplike trance.

Mr. Brackstone's psyche drifted back in time, back to when he was just a boy. The home he grew up in was cold and unloving. The children in town made fun of Mr. Brackstone on a daily basis. He was exceptionally slender, and most of the girls in town could beat him up if they so desired. Mr. Brackstone brandished nicknames of all harsh calibers. The most demeaning of them turned out to be the favorite of most of the popular children. They spoke out in ostracizing unison, viciously calling him names like "Cuntboy Clifford."

This mind-numbing name would send Mr. Brackstone into an immediate cry fest, and the local boys couldn't get enough. So like most chastised children, little Clifford spent most of his time at home with his nose stuck into books. However, the books at his house were not the usual reading material of a small-town family. Mr. Brackstone's father and mother were bizarre people. They hardly ever addressed their son. When they did, it was to chastise him or give him a solid beating.

His father was a tall man, built very lean, and extremely pitiless. He worked at the local mortuary embalming the dead. He kept books of that morbid nature in the home as reference material for work. When Mr. Brackstone was just five years old, his father began to sit him on his lap and show him the pictures from the mortuary manuals, pointing out the most gruesome and horrible examples of death. When Mr. Brackstone cried, his father would jab him in the ribs until he stopped. Eventually, Mr. Brackstone grew numb to the beatings and the pictures. He grew fascinated by the books and no longer feared the disgusting images. When his father noticed that he did not get upset with his taunting anymore, he left Mr. Brackstone alone altogether. As weird as his father was, he was a saint compared to his repulsive mother.

Mr. Brackstone's mother was an odd-looking creature. She was awfully dumpy in build, with a disgusting large calcified hump on her back. Her disability made her hunch over when she walked. She wore bifocals to offset her crossed eyes and dragged her feet as she lumbered around the house. Her white vascular hands were disgustingly turned out from severe arthritis. She usually wore black sweats with old worn-out house shoes for weeks on end. As unbelievable as it seemed, her decrepit looks matched her cruel behavior.

Mr. Brackstone's mind went back to one particular October morning. He was ten years old. The bight of frost was in the morning air as little Clifford woke up to his parents screaming at each other as usual. He heard his father chastising his mother about her looks and the way she kept the home in such shambles. His beast of a mother lashed back with her own insults toward his father. Finally, his father had enough. An earsplitting slap echoed down the hallway into Clifford's room, and a thud followed. Clifford heard the front door open and slam shut. His father drove off to work in his rusty Buick, leaving him alone with her. Like most abusers of children, his mother was an opportunist of seclusion. Her awful intrusions always happened when they were alone, when he had no defense against her.

Clifford pulled his soiled blanket up over his terrified face. He thought if he could pretend to be asleep, she might leave him be. Panic took over his body. Clifford shivered underneath the blanket in fear of what was to come. At that point in time, he could hear his mother dragging her feet down the hallway. Her heavy steps grew closer, announcing her devilish, impending presence. A shrieking voice screamed orders through the thin bedroom wall.

"Clifford! Clifford! You better be ready for school, you little bastard, or so help me, I'll kill you!"

Clifford leaped out of bed and looked at the clock—7:30 a.m.

Oh my god, no! he said to himself, realizing how late he was.

He was so scared listening to his parents' fight that he had forgotten to get ready for school. Feverishly, Clifford pulled off his pajamas, trying to beat his mother's footsteps, which were already halfway down the hall. The heavy pulls of soiled house shoes dragging along the hallway counted down the mere seconds left before her unwelcome morning entrance. Clifford stood bare naked as his mother rounded the hallway into his room. The young boy froze in fear, holding a pair of socks in one hand and his Hanes briefs in the other.

Exposed and senseless, Clifford continued his futile attempt to get dressed in time for school. His mother forced herself upon him in a fit of rage. She hacked away relentlessly with her withered hands at Clifford's naked body. Her freakish green fingernails tore at his soft, youthful flesh like a rusty saw through soft pinewood. His pitiful screams echoed down the hallway to no avail. After her hands grew tired and weary, she kicked him harshly in the stomach. Clifford doubled over in pain and curled up in the fetal position. The beating that ensued lasted only moments more, but it seemed like an eternity to the pitiful ten-year-old victim. As she slammed her last kicks into his rib cage, the hunchback witch sucked up every ounce of mucus in her throat and spit a huge yellow-and-green booger-infested slimeball on his face.

"You are a useless piece of trash, and you will never amount to anything. Get up and get ready for school, you little fucker, before I really give you something to cry about."

Clifford sat up, wiping the mucus ball from his youthful face as he vigorously pleaded, "I'm sorry, Momma. Please don't hit me anymore. I won't cry anymore!"

"You're lucky I don't kill your worthless ass. What are you worth, huh? You don't help out around here. You only cause problems. You are a worthless man just like your father. You won't amount to shit."

The young boy wiped streaming tears from his eyes and struggled to his feet.

"I'm sorry, Momma. I won't do it again."

His mother watched as he struggled to stand up straight. Large bruises already permeated Clifford's fragile body as a result of the beating he had just taken. She bent down and took Clifford by the wrist.

Shaking his entire body, she uttered, "Look at you. You are disgustingly skinny and weak. You are a terrible excuse for a boy. I think you would be better off if I just pulled them off, Clifford."

The merciless hunchback forcefully took a hold of his prepubescent testicles. Then, she squeezed them tightly with her cruel hand and harsh intentions.

"What do you think I should do, Clifford? Should I pull them off?"

Clifford agonized in pain and pleaded with his mother, "No. Please, Mother! Don't do that. I swear I'll be good. I won't be late anymore. Please don't pull them off!"

The heartless harpy looked at her scrawny son with repugnance then dug her jagged nails deep into his miniature ball sack. Soft, pliable flesh grinded under her dreadful claws. Clifford screamed and collapsed to the floor. Tugging and grinding her fingers deeper and deeper, she took her only son to new levels of pain. He curled up in a tight ball and cried recklessly for hours, with no one to comfort him and no one to ever come to his rescue. The young boy abandoned reality and escaped to the furthest reaches of the human mind, where no one can physically hurt you, where a person drives themselves insane. The thoughts of his childhood streamed through his mind like a never-ending nightmare.

Colette looked on in shock. Clifford soulfully cried real tears and begged his mother for mercy, unaware of what time and place he was in. The pain was the same to him. The memory stampeded through his twisted brain, overtaking his grip on reality. And Colette found herself watching her abductor, fearfully wondering what made him into this crazed creature that presently held her hostage.

Chapter 17

Revelation

MILDRED PULLED UP TO MR. Brackstone's house in hurried antic-ipation. She yanked out her federal-issue Glock nine millimeter and hung her FBI badge loosely around her neck on a long silver chain. Cautiously looking through the front window into the filth that was the Brackstone residence, Mildred saw light from the back porch sneaking through the back door and into the kitchen. Moving around the side of the house through the heavy brush, she caught an awful scent. At once, she grabbed her nose defensively. The smell of rancid food and God knows what else hit her in the face and invaded her sinuses. Mildred broke off a cigarette into two pieces and put each one up her nose—an old trick she had picked up while working crime-scene crowds for the more experienced agents.

She suspiciously entered the filthy home. Adrenaline picked up, pushing a surge of energy down her arms and into her metallic pis-tol. Thrusting her Glock in front of her around every turn, Mildred slowly gazed upon every crevice and dark corner, expecting to find Mr. Brackstone waiting for her in the shadows. The kitchen felt cold and dirty. Her natural reflexes told her to get far away, but her train-ing pushed her farther into the house. She came to Mr. Brackstone's bedroom. It looked rummaged through, like someone left in a hurry. She looked to the dresser top; it was covered in dirt. Though she noticed a good number of small rectangular breaks in the dust.

"What did you take with you, Mr. Brackstone?" Mildred asked herself as she inspected the dresser drawers.

Piles of old molded trash and clothing littered the ground. Every new crunching step disgusted her. She tried not to disturb any of it, in case evidence was hiding somewhere inside the piles of filth. Everywhere she stepped drew crunches of old chips and snacks or squirts of rancid liquid through the old shag carpet.

Mildred made her way to the bottom of the staircase. A new smell forced its way past the tobacco. She had smelled it before. It was the unmistakable odor of death.

"Hello? Is anyone up there? Is anyone hurt? This is the FBI. I'm here to help!" Mildred hollered sternly up the poorly lit steps.

The vile smell led her to the attic. With her gun thrusting forward, she entered the miniscule upper room.

"Oh my god, no!" she screamed.

Seeing her very own Father Conner hunched over dead on the floor, Mildred suddenly had a new definition for the word *grief*. The fresh smell of death and the sight of her longtime friend and mentor sprawled out on the floor forced her stomach to clinch. At first, she fought off the gag reflex, holding her hand over her mouth and swallowing. A second look through her tangled hair at Father Conner in such an awful state sent another ominous wave over her. She could not fight it off this time. Mildred puked all over herself. Small pieces of partially digested spaghetti and tomato sauce trickled down her chin and onto her blouse. She wiped the final warm chunks of vomit away from her chin and sheepishly lifted her head. Looking up with tears in her bloodshot eyes, Mildred embraced cruel reality and let out a howl of sorrow. She crawled to the old priest's leg, sobbing like a newly informed war widow. Mildred sat next to Father Conner, holding his head against her vomit-covered bosom.

"It's okay, Father Conner. You rest now. I'm so sorry. I shouldn't have said anything to you. You were too smart, you figured it out, didn't you? You came over here to see the monster for yourself, and you paid with your life. It should have been me on the floor, not you. I would have walked into this trap before you. You did not deserve to die like this."

Mildred wiped the tears from her eyes and looked up as if she was speaking to God directly.

"It should have been me, not Father Conner! Why did you take the only good man that I have ever known? Why did you have to make a monster like Mr. Cliff Brackstone? Why did you put me on this fucking earth to live this miserable life where nothing ever turns out well for anyone and the only people who get ahead are the ones who do wrong? Well, I don't care. I am going to find Mr. Brackstone, and I am going to kill him. Not for you. Not for justice. I am going to do it for me and all of his victims and, most of all, for this good man who did not deserve to die this horrible death!"

She picked up her cell phone and pushed her emergency call button.

"This is Agent Mildred Beron requesting a full CSI team and a lead agent on my position, over."

A static voice responded within seconds, "*Agent Beron, we have you as inactive and on leave. Please report the nature of your request, over.*"

Mildred looked down at Father Conner's dead body and around the satanically decorated room then replied in an utterly disgusted tone, "The nature of my request involves a dead priest, an ass-backwards town, a sorry-ass agent who couldn't save a friend, and probably one of the sickest fucking serial killers since John Wayne fucking Gacy! So I suggest you take my call seriously and get some people out here, over."

There was no way of handling it on her own now. Her delusions of a self-serving revenge had been his downfall. Mr. Brackstone had undoubtedly fled. Father Conner had been murdered, and she was about to face an FBI task force. In less than an hour, she will have to try to explain the secret she's been keeping for so long, how it led to the death of Father Conner and the escape of Mr. Brackstone. This will most assuredly cost her the only thing pumping blood through her veins: the chance of violent vindication by her own hands.

CHAPTER 18

First Date

COLETTE WAS SCRUNCHED UP ON the cold wooden floor, hatefully peering at her depraved abductor. Her fists remained poised, ready for his advance. The time for crying and whimpering had passed. She could either fight or give in. Mr. Brackstone sat on the cot across the room from her. His prized pictures lay scattered around the room from the initial fight. Small pieces of glass from one of the broken picture frames glistened on the floor like millions of miniature diamonds. Mr. Brackstone looked into Colette's eyes in a psychotic fashion, searching for the first signs of weakness. He licked his thin, pasty lips and watched with his empty eyes, probing meticulously, as a scavenger would while waiting for a wounded animal to lose all its strength.

Mr. Brackstone opened his duffel bag and pulled out a gallon jug of water. He poured himself a large glass of the cool fluid, taunting Colette with every sip of the crystal clear liquid. Her mouth was beginning to dry up. She could barely get her teeth wet with her tongue. Drinking the refreshing water down about halfway, he heinously poured the rest of it onto the wooden floor. The water trickled close to Colette, staining the old dusty wood. Colette thrust her fingers at the moist ground then back to her lips, trying to gather up some moisture. Mr. Brackstone smirked at her then let out an evil laugh.

"Fuck you. You sick bastard. You'll never take me. Do you hear me? Never!" Colette screamed at the top of her voice, pulling at the unbreakable knots which kept her fastened to the wall.

Mr. Brackstone simply sat still and laughed.

"How the mighty have fallen. Oh, you can yell and scream as much as you want, no one will hear you way up here. Well, nobody besides all the bats in the belfries."

A light went off in Colette's mind. She now realized where she was.

The old clock tower, she whispered to herself in surprise.

Directly in the center of Riverside, where Main Street meets River Road, the town had an old watch factory from the fifties. The architecture of the building was like that of an old Gothic German fort. At the top of the twenty-story building, there was an old four-faced clock, the kind of town clock you only see in Europe. Nonetheless, the clock tower resided in Riverside. The factory shut down sometime ago, but the town had recently started the clock back up to give Riverside a more "likable" atmosphere.

All those noises she had heard were the gears grinding together. She thought of how high the tower was and realized Mr. Brackstone was right. She could scream with a bullhorn in the little room that entrapped her, and no one on the street would even remotely hear her. The reality of her desperate situation began to sink in. Her capturer was right; she would soon grow tired, too tired to fight back. Then he was going to take whatever he wanted.

"Why are you doing this, Mr. Brackstone? I never did anything to you. I was always a good student. So why the hell are you doing this to me?" the defiant hostage asked in a disgusted manner.

"Why indeed? I will tell you why, Colette. You should feel lucky. You are the first of my victims to ever hear this before I take what I want. Are you ready for the truth?"

Colette shook her head in acceptance.

"It's like this, Ms. Jennings: All of my life, I have been picked on, made fun of, even ridiculed for my...well, let's say...'unlucky' genetics. The things my mother did to me should have killed me a long time ago, but I survived. The way I grew up should have killed me, but I survived. As I got older and began to study science, I read about a man named Darwin. He spoke only truths to me. I embraced his philosophies of life and death. His teachings consumed

79

me, turned me into what you see today. Darwin's theory is a simple one: only the strong will survive. I am a true child of Darwin, Ms. Jennings, the next in a great line of evolutionary change. I take what I want through the power of the mind. I outwit, outsmart, and out-think people. Therefore, I am stronger. I am the ultimate survivor, Colette. I am the future!"

Mr. Brackstone looked at Colette with a victorious glimmer on his face and then pointed to her with his long pale fingers. He exploded in a fit of newfound rage, screaming like a self-glorified preacher.

"*You* are the perfect unforgiving scum of this earth, happy in your pleasant existence, mocking me with every giggle and smirk. I piss on your perfect world. I shit on your unblemished existence. I am the strong one, not you! *I* am the predator, and you are the prey."

Colette was shocked for a moment by Mr. Brackstone's outburst. She saw the pure hatred and psychopathic nature of her one-time mild-mannered science teacher. Gathering her wits about her, she decided she wasn't going to play along and be the helpless victim. If she had any chance of getting out of this alive, she had to get him close while she still had the strength to overcome him.

Rising to her feet with a rebellious tone, Colette uttered, "That is the biggest load of crap I have ever heard in my life! You think you are stronger than others because you lurk in the shadows like a rat and pick off the weakest people you can find."

Mr. Brackstone's face turned beet red, and his fists clenched. He wiped his mouth and whispered, "Shut up, you little bitch."

"Oh, what's the matter, little momma's boy? Can dish it out but can't take it? That's right, you little bitch. I already kicked your skinny, pale, freaky-looking ass all over this room. A *girl* kicked your ass! I wonder what Darwin would say about that. That's not strong. That's pathetic!"

Colette screamed out her taunting insults while crouched in a guard position. Mr. Brackstone stood up on the cot, infuriated.

"Shut up, you bitch!"

Mr. Brackstone lunged at Colette like a starving coon on a trash heap. His scrawny frame flew across the room at an astounding velocity. The first thing he saw was Colette's glimmering smile. He came down to the floor and felt a sharp pain then a shortness of breath. Colette karate-chopped him in the throat. She knew she had to keep him close, so she wheeled Mr. Brackstone around then landed a one-two combination to his face. Mr. Brackstone hit the ground, shocked. Before he could get to his feet, she was on him again. A swift kick to the ribs drew his breath out of his chest. Another to the groin doubled him over in severe pain.

Mr. Brackstone's chances of getting out of this were slipping further away with every ensuing kick. He grabbed the closest rope to him and tugged as hard as he could. Colette crashed to the ground as the rope strapped to her left ankle pulled her leg across the room. She landed right next to Mr. Brackstone; their eyes locked for a second. The sick-minded demon lunged forward with his jagged yellow teeth exposed. He plunged his hideous fangs into Colette's right cheek and clamped down, tearing into her supple flesh until he tasted her salty blood in his mouth. She wedged both of her thumbs harshly into his eye sockets and forced his teeth off her face. The heroic hostage continued to jam her thumbnails deep into his eyes, trying with all her might to blind him.

Mr. Brackstone squealed in pain. He felt overpowered. Rearing both of his hands back, he brutally brought them together on Colette's delicate ears. The harsh impact caught her off guard. A loud buzz echoed inside her head. With another swift boxing of her ears, Mr. Brackstone managed to free his face from her menacing grip. Colette's vision blurred, and she tried to regain her equilibrium to launch another attack. But Mr. Brackstone's will to survive was too great. He had already made it back to his feet by the time she drew her fist back.

The flimsy murderer kicked her in the chest and sent her crashing to the floor. He landed another swift boot to her ribs and squawked, "Is that all you have to offer, Ms. Jennings?"

At that moment, Colette became a wild animal. She lunged forward with her bloody face and locked her powerful jaws onto Mr. Brackstone's inner thigh, biting down so hard the small room echoed with a hideous crunching sound. Mr. Brackstone's eyes rolled back into his head as he yelped like a wounded dog. He sprawled down on top of her and forced her to the ground. To his dismay, she did not let go of her horrid bite. In fact, she wrenched her teeth even deeper. Mr. Brackstone writhed in pain but could not dislodge the attacking student from his inner thigh. He pounded on her back with his insignificant slaps and punches, losing more and more strength by the second. Colette took a deep breath in through her bloody nose and clamped down again. She could feel her canines beginning to touch one another, and Mr. Brackstone's warm blood flowed heavily into her mouth.

Mr. Brackstone grew frantic. He scurried his hands to the back of her shorts and forced them down over her ass. Then with the malevolence of a medieval sadist, he jammed his thumb into her rectum. The sudden shock of it forced Colette to loosen her bite. Because of Mr. Brackstone's long thumbnail rooting through the easily ripped inner walls of her rectum, it felt as though someone had jammed a rusty nail into her anus. She threw herself backward, dislodging Mr. Brackstone's thumb and freeing him at the same time.

Mr. Brackstone quickly scurried to his soiled cot once again, doubled over in pain. Colette backed up against the wall, holding her bloody cheek with one hand and pulling her shorts up with the other. She wondered if that was her last chance at freedom.

"Bravo, Ms. Jennings. I didn't know you had it in you to be so primal. Oh, that really turns me on."

Colette, still being defiant, lunged at Mr. Brackstone, only to be snapped back by the medieval-looking ropes tied to the wall.

She said, "You sorry son of a bitch, get back over here. I will finish you off once and for all. Come on! Darwin wouldn't just sit there and watch. He would be a real man and try to take me again."

"Oh no, Ms. Jennings. I will wait it out. I am very impressed by your vigor though. The harder you fight against those ropes, the sooner you will be totally out of energy."

Mr. Brackstone got as close to Colette as he could without stepping within her groping reach. The two adversaries were almost nose to nose, and Mr. Brackstone uttered another despicable rant.

"I can't wait to take you, Colette Jennings. I can't wait to hear you scream my name."

CHAPTER 19

Call in the Troops

MILDRED SAT IN MELANCHOLY SORROW by Father Conner's grotesque corpse. She reluctantly made the call to FBI headquarters and the local police department. Soon the house would be crawling with local yokels who had never seen a murder. The stench of death permeated the air. Mildred perched on both knees then made a solemn oath as she was looking into the lifeless eyes of the old man.

"I swear by the end of this, by my will, I will not stop until he is destroyed. Wherever he goes, I will follow. I will chase him to the ends of the earth if need be. To finish this, I swear on my life that Mr. Cliff Brackstone will never kill an innocent person again."

The echoing sirens grew closer. The police pulled into the driveway and onto the yard. They kicked in the front door then rushed the house as if it were a murder in progress. The locals' quick sweep of the place found Mildred with Father Conner in the attic. One of the new deputies puked at the sight and smell of the dead priest.

"Get him the hell away from the crime scene!" Mildred shouted as she rushed the police out of the attic.

Mildred forced the local police out of the home and onto the front porch. She gathered them together and gave them a quick hit description of the man they were looking for. It was kind of pointless, considering the cops all knew the teaching staff at the high school, being such a small town. No sooner had the local cops start to scatter than up pulled a black Chevy Caprice with government tags.

A tall black man stepped out of the car. He was sharply dressed in a dark-blue Hugo Boss suit. He had large light-brown eyes and a tendency to smirk almost as if it were a nervous twitch. His skin was light brown and seemed to shine off the florescent glow of the street-lights. He walked up to the porch with a cowboy swagger, revealing his FBI badge over his left front pocket. He hopped up to the front door and turned to face the crowd of local Riverside police. In a smooth yet confident manner, he addressed the men.

"Gentlemen, my name is FBI Special Agent Andre Branch. This is now an official FBI crime scene, which makes it *my* crime scene. All of you deputies that rallied in here peeling wheels on the lawn ruined possible evidence. All of you who searched through the inside of this house ruined possible evidence. All of you who messed with, looked at, or breathed on the murder victim ruined possible evidence. So from now on, you do not fart, sneeze, wink, cry, talk, touch, or even get close to my crime scene. Now, someone tape this area off, because the time we are wasting could be ruining possible evidence."

He entered the house soon after his little speech, confident he had instilled the fear of God into the local department. He motioned for Mildred to follow him. Branch slipped a pair of surgical gloves on then looked over the house. Mildred went in right after him.

"So, Agent Beron, what do we have?" he asked Mildred.

Looking shocked that Branch knew her name, she nervously replied, "One murder victim up in the attic, possible traps through-out the house, a probable psychopathic serial killer on the loose."

Branch looked at her with severity at the words "possible serial killer."

"And you just let this probable psychopath get away clean, huh?" Branch retorted.

Mildred shifted her eyes to the floor in embarrassment.

"No, sir, I was not here to stop this. I did not realize the serious-ness of the situation until I did some investigation. And by the time I got here, it was too late. I take full responsibility."

"You can save the full-responsibility bull for the boys at head-quarters. I don't need a bunch of academy talk here, Agent. What

I need is your full input on the situation. The real input, not some watered-down version you think will get your ass out of trouble. Now let me take a look at this crime scene."

They both walked up the old creaking stairs to the attic. Branch inspected the long rusted nails piercing through the old priest's tender flesh. Then he looked at the priest. His careful motions showed the experience of a longtime FBI field veteran. He wasted no movement. His cool hand technique had given him the respect of his peers, plus the ability to catch over twenty murderers in his tenure. Branch pulled out a small disposable camera and shot pictures of the crime scene from every angle he could. He collected samples of blood from the priest. Then, he pulled Mildred out of the room and locked the door behind him. Branch looked at Mildred with his light-brown eyes and put his hands on her shoulders.

"Mildred, this is an exceptionally big mess. From what I've heard from my superiors, you believe this Mr. Cliff Brackstone is a serial killer. You told Langley that you already have some evidence of over twenty possible victims. You let these local fuckups fuck up my crime scene. Now you are sitting here as silent as a little kid on Christmas night. Why in the hell are you not saying a damn word about what's going on? Now, you can either tell me what's happening around here, or I can send your ass back to Langley with a filing cabinet full of misconduct and misprocedure papers that will put your ass on the bench for this entire thing. Then the uptight boys down in Virginia can get the details out of you."

Mildred looked shocked that he would come at her like that. She thought about calling him every name in the book but regained her composure. She sat down on the stairs; her bloodshot eyes misted with heavy tears. It was nearly impossible to catch her breath and speak. She proceeded to tell Agent Branch the entire story, how she was raped as a child by Mr. Cliff Brackstone, how she didn't feel like she was the only one, how she had come back to Riverside on a crusade to stop him. Branch looked at Mildred with pity for a second then with disgust after it had sunk in. He picked up his cell phone and quickly called headquarters.

"We have a possible multiple-victim situation here. A suspected serial killer on the loose. I need a full team down to Riverside as soon as possible. I need an APB on a one Mr. Cliff Brackstone, white male between thirty and forty years of age, five foot nine and approximately one hundred and fifty pounds. He is to be considered armed and extremely dangerous!"

Walking back down the mud-saturated stairs, Mildred looked at her reflection in the window. Her hair was a thick black tangled mess. She had soiled clothing on, and her face was covered in dirt. Her tears streaked through the dark dust on her face, creating small roadways of clean white skin on one side and dark-red birthmark on the other.

Mildred wandered outside and sat down on the front porch. Her inner thoughts questioning whether she could have done anything different. What if she had known how deep Mr. Brackstone's evil was and how many girls he had taken advantage of? She could have told somebody about him instead of trying to deal with it herself. The lonely police file faces of the girls from the missing-person reports flashed through her tired mind. She wondered what had become of the others, the Nothing Girls. Just as she was about to break down into a full-fledged female sob, Special Agent Branch joined her on the front porch.

"I talked to HQ. They don't want to pull you yet, but only because I talked them out of it. You are to fill out a complete report on everything you know, and I mean down to the last sick detail. I don't care how personal it is, we need all the information. I need you crispy on this one. We are going to be working together. So go back to your hotel, get cleaned up, and for God's sakes, get some sleep. We will deal with this maniac when you wake up."

With that said, Branch hopped off the porch directing the local police how to block off the area. Mildred stood up and dusted herself off. She started walking to her car when, all of a sudden, there was a buzz among the local boys in blue. They all seemed energized and up in arms. She could see Branch talking to one of the local cops and then taking off as quick as he came. Mildred grabbed one of the deputies and inquired about what was going on. The deputy told her the news that had just come in off the radio.

"A girl is missing from Riverside High. Her name is Colette Jennings, and the last person she was seen with was Mr. Cliff Brackstone."

Hatred filled in her powerful eyes. Mildred could not believe what was happening. The demon she had come to stop was winning the battle. All her dreams of bringing Mr. Brackstone to justice seemed like empty feelings. Her heroic stance had now become her worst nightmare, and the self-serving method of revenge she had planned just landed another victim in her demented adversary's evil grasp.

CHAPTER 20

I See You

THE TOP OF THE GOTHIC clock tower was built historically to resemble an old brick castle fortress. Tall stone walls extend high above the rooftop with breaks between the pillars above the windows. Perched on top of the old clock tower roof, hidden behind the old archer's divider, Mr. Brackstone looked at his dwelling through a high-powered telescope meant for stargazing. He saw the blue-and-yellow police cars with their lights flashing. The officers looked frantic and ran about as if their hurried pace could change the recent events. A monstrous grin materialized across his pasty lips, but a painful frown soon reformed from the stitch in his ribs. Colette's brutal kicks still had Mr. Brackstone doubled over in pain. But watching the police scramble and wander around the city gave Mr. Brackstone a feeling of triumph. It soothed his aching body and relaxed him for a moment. He felt as if he had fooled the entire town all these years into thinking he was harmless. Now they would see the truth. Mr. Brackstone's revelry in the moment could only be thought of as pure bliss through his distorted mind.

"Finally, all of my work is going to be noticed. I will no longer be just another forgotten face in the lingering crowd. People will fear me. Who knows, they might even make a movie out of this," he said to himself with an inflated chest.

However, as every moment of happiness went in Mr. Brackstone's life, it did not last long. The lights of the flashing police cars became hypnotic to him, his eyes glazed over, and then he sank back into one of the dark corners of the rooftop. He fixed his telescope once again on his home. A muscular police dog blurred past his ocular lens and trounced through his front yard, tugging a skinny deputy officer behind. Mr. Brackstone became fixated on the sleek German shepherd. His sick happiness seemed to fade from his face as he thought back into his childhood to one of the only times he was truly happy.

Seeing the mammoth dog jogged Mr. Brackstone's memory of his best boyhood friend. When Mr. Brackstone was eleven years old, he found a German shepherd puppy wandering the green acres of Riverside. When local families had to move or got tired of their dogs for whatever reason, they would usually ditch them in the state-protected land to fend for themselves. This particular puppy was close to death from starvation. Young Mr. Brackstone scooped up the famished animal and immediately took it home.

His cruel mother didn't seem to care, but secretly she knew this would be another way to torture and control her son in the future, especially if he fell in love with the adorable puppy, as most boys do. So Mr. Brackstone slowly but surely nursed the dog back to health. Every day, he hand-fed his needy beast and gave it the utmost affection. Finally, when the puppy was nursed back to full health, he named it Sam. From that day forward, Mr. Brackstone had finally made a true friend. Everywhere Mr. Brackstone went, Sam followed. Not only was he a great companion to Mr. Brackstone; he was also his only escape from his cruel reality.

Sam grew up fast. He turned out to be an incredibly large brute and extremely loyal to Mr. Brackstone. His large snout protruded out ominously, draped in a tan color leading up to a black mask of fur that ran straight down his back. Long legs riddled with long muscle and shaped down into his paws that housed exceptionally menacing-looking, shadowy claws. Clean white fangs that would leave a shark jealous dangled between his powerful jaws, threatening any aggressor through sheer intimidation.

All of a sudden, the local bullies who once found it easy to pick on Mr. Brackstone for a good laugh now thought twice with Sam by his side. Even at school, the cruel kids decided it wasn't such a good idea to rough Mr. Brackstone up anymore for fear of his ever-looming, white-fanged protector. The only thing that got Mr. Brackstone through his boring school days and the terrible waking nightmares of his mother that year was the thought of seeing Sam when he got home.

Mr. Brackstone's memory took him back to the tragic day that changed his life forever. The sun could barely be seen behind an ill-omened gray sky. It rained off and on all day, making the air heavy and the ground moist. Mr. Brackstone wandered home after his arduously boring day. Jogging down the wet avenue, he covered his slight body from the light drizzle with one of his obtuse US history books. He could see Sam's inviting K-9 grin from down the street. His lumbering friend stood patiently on all fours, waiting tolerantly for Mr. Brackstone to arrive home. Sam wagged his tail, shaking muddy rainwater all over because he was soaked to the bone. His wet fur hung down his strong body in clumps of dripping mass. Sam wasn't allowed in the house because his mother said quite often, "One male loser is all the house can stand at one time."

Mr. Brackstone excitedly opened the fence, and Sam greeted him with a warm lick to his laughing face. The large shepherd placed both paws to Mr. Brackstone's chest, covering the overjoyed boy with mud. Sam pawed and licked him at least ten times, showing his undying affection for the boy. Mr. Brackstone laughed like any eleven-year-old boy would and then proceeded to roughhouse with Sam in the backyard for what seemed like hours. The thought of it being wet outside or getting dirty didn't bother Mr. Brackstone. He just wanted to play with his best friend after a long outcast day at school. Mr. Brackstone and Sam played as free and happy as only children and their dogs could. Sam barked and chased him until they were both exhausted from joy. Then, Mr. Brackstone heard the unwelcome sound of his mother's car pulling into the driveway.

He quickly looked at his mud-covered watch; the dim florescent light flashed 5:30 p.m. He had been so wrapped up in playing with Sam that he lost track of time. Mr. Brackstone looked down at his clothes.

"Oh no," he tearfully whispered to himself.

Seeing that he was covered in mud and dog hair, he desperately tried to clean some of the mud off his jacket and pants before she could see. But his futile efforts came too late.

"Clifford Brackstone. What have you been doing, you little dirty son of a bastard?" his hunchback mother screamed from the back door, looking at Mr. Brackstone soaked standing next to Sam.

Mr. Brackstone cowered, slumped his shoulders, and dropped his head. All the joy he had just been enthralled with seemed like a distant memory now. He knew this was going to bring a harsh beating. Mr. Brackstone begrudgingly walked to the backdoor. His mother's hunchback frame hovered over him as he entered the house. She was so furious Mr. Brackstone could feel her hot panting breath on the back of his neck as he passed her through the doorway. Before he could get into the house, his cruel beast of a mother was on him.

She bitch-slapped the soaked child to the cold kitchen floor. As he turned to face her, he could hear the sound of the utensil drawer opening. Scurrying to his feet, he saw his mother grasping a heavy wooden rolling pin. She swung the unmerciful piece of wood, smashing Mr. Brackstone in the side of his face. An explosion of blood erupted on Mr. Brackstone's cheek as he once again went crashing to the hard tile floor. He could taste the salty blood dripping out of his mouth. Mr. Brackstone's hunchback mother barked an outraged order, "Take those filthy clothes off, you no-good bastard! Take them off or I'll rip them off of you!"

As Mr. Brackstone undressed, his mother wiped the rolling pin clean with a paper towel. Mr. Brackstone took all his clothes off, besides his undershorts, and lay on the cold tile floor, holding himself and shivering in fear. His mother slowly dragged her feet closer to him. The hunchback demon had a look in her eyes that could turn a man to solid stone. Mr. Brackstone began to warily beg and plead with his mother not to hurt him.

"No, Mother, please stop hurting me. It won't happen again. I'll clean it all up, I swear. Just please don't hurt me!"

The lingering monster ignored her boy's moving request. Licking her thin, pasty lips, she neared the scurrying boy, saying in her haggard voice, "You will never forget this as long as you live, Clifford.

91

You are just like all the men in this world. You're dirty, filthy, and you don't deserve mercy. I am going to teach you a hard lesson today. A lesson you will never forget, I promise you that much."

The pitiless ogre pounced on the scrawny boy with surprising speed, pinning him to the floor. Then she struck him fiercely with a solid blow from the rolling pin to the young boy's scrawny chest. All the air in Mr. Brackstone's chest rushed out immediately. He horribly gasped for air. Mr. Brackstone couldn't think of anything to do. Utter despair filled his young heart, as he was thinking surely she would kill him this time. As she reared back with the rolling pin once more, Mr. Brackstone instinctively screamed out for the only friend he had in the world, "Sam, help! Sam, help me!"

Before his mother could bat an eyelash, the monstrous black German shepherd crashed through the screen door and sank his razor-sharp teeth into her arm. The ferocious dog attacked as if it had been waiting decades to unleash its full force on Mr. Brackstone's monstrous mother. The young boy witnessed a frozen look on his mother's face he had never seen before. The hunchback beast that showed no emotion whatsoever was shocked and afraid. Sam threw his head back and forth at an incredible rate of speed, digging his jagged teeth deeper into the deformed hunchback's forearm. She screamed and pleaded with Mr. Brackstone to call Sam off.

"Clifford! Call him off! Please! He is trying to kill me!"

Crazed with blind emotional instinct, Sam ripped and tugged at her arms, sinking his canines deeper into her soft flesh. Mr. Brackstone backed up against the nearest wall and called Sam to him. The large animal released the shocked hunchback woman and walked over to his master's side.

"I'm bleeding, oh my god, I am bleeding so badly!" Mr. Brackstone's mother exclaimed as she grasped at the open wounds on her wrist. She looked at Mr. Brackstone and Sam in fear for her life and subsequently, nervously reached for a butcher knife from her utensil drawer.

"You keep that thing away from me, Clifford! Do you hear me? You keep it away! I'm going to call the police now. They will destroy that thing," she said with a stern tone, attempting to regain control of the situation.

Sam lifted his jowls and showed his bloody teeth. Mr. Brackstone's young face turned sour and uncaring. The child in him had just died a venomous death. A look of evil that few men have ever attained took over Mr. Brackstone's entire demeanor. He stared down his hunchback mother with the hatred only years of physical and mental abuse can breed. The hunchback dragged herself over the thin wall and toiled to her feet. She picked up the wall-mounted phone and dialed the police. Sobbing into the phone about how her son's dog had gone crazy, she gave them her address and hung up.

"I don't think they're going to make it in time to help you, Mother," Mr. Brackstone said with an evil grin as he let go of Sam's collar, happily ordering him to attack. Sam leaped across the room. He locked his heavy jaws against the soft, fragile skin of her throat, sending the hunchback crashing to the floor. She swung her butcher knife, plunging it into Sam's side several times. As each second passed, her attempts to fight for her life grew less. Sam's long fangs worked themselves deep into her throat. Blood gushed from her arteries, turning the once-solid white tile floor into a solid red pool of blood. Sam's large head thrashed back and forth, dragging Mr. Brackstone's mother across the floor while smashing her head off the knee-high cabinets. In only a matter of seconds, the struggle ended. An eerie snap filled the room as Sam's powerful jaws finally worked their way past her tendons and flesh and to the bone. The black shepherd's powerful jaws broke her fragile neck like a dried twig.

Mr. Brackstone looked on somberly as his dog released his mother's lifeless body. Then, Sam fell down beside her. Mr. Brackstone hurried over to Sam's side.

"That's a good boy, Sam. You're the only friend I've ever had. I will never forget this."

Sam licked his master's face, covering his cheek in his mother's fresh blood, then died in Mr. Brackstone's arms. As Mr. Brackstone knelt on the blood-soaked kitchen floor, he looked at the gaping wound in his mother's neck. No sorrow reflected on his face, only relief that his mother was dead. Mr. Brackstone was happy she was dead. The monster that gave him regular mental and physical beatings was gone. A new Mr. Cliff Brackstone manifested that cloud-covered, rainy day in the heart of suburbia.

All shades of emotion and love Mr. Brackstone had in his body died when Sam died. He was now completely alone, a shell of a human. The only thing left was hatred and spite.

The eleven-year-old boy looked at his mother one last time, saying, "You're right, Mother... I will never forget this day as long as I live."

CHAPTER 21

Search

THE HEARTBREAKING NEWS OF COLETTE's kidnapping spread like wildfire throughout the small town. Everyone was in complete shock. It wasn't long before Tom and Mat heard the horrible news. Mat took it terribly, feeling at fault personally because she was his girlfriend and, therefore, his responsibility.

"I cannot believe I let this happen. What kind of man am I, Tom?"

"It's not your fault, man. Look, I feel just as bad. Nobody knew anything about this. How could you stop something you never saw coming?"

"That's just it, Tom. I always felt there was something creepy about that weirdo Mr. Brackstone. I should have never let her out of my sight around him. Why didn't I just stay with her? I'm going to kill that son of a bitch if he touches her!"

Tom put his hand on Mat's shoulders, attempting to calm his irate friend down.

"Standing here talking shit about it isn't going to get us any-where, Mat. Now let's get started and see how we can help out on this thing, okay?"

The boys decided to gather forces and search for her in town. They flew down the old back roads in Tom's old beat-up Chevy truck, not knowing where to start or what to do. Mat felt his high self-esteem deflate since the news hit him. His inner ego kept telling him he was supposed to be her protector, her champion.

The story was not supposed to go like this in Mat's mind. If there was ever any trouble, he was supposed to be there to save her, not search for her with no idea of where to find her while she lay helpless somewhere at some psychopath's discretion. Tom's bitter face looked worried as well. His mind wondered on the horrible things that could be happening to his longtime companion. He found his emotions leading him to feel more scared than angry, aimlessly racing around the backstreets of Riverside with Mat, trying to find a figurative needle in the haystack.

Finally, the boys stopped the truck down by the Delaware River. Infuriated, Mat stomped out of the truck, cursing and hurling rocks into the choppy water. Tom followed him out of the truck.

"Well, Tom, I don't know what we are going to do now. I have no idea where else we can look. She isn't in any of the local hiding spots we know about. We are going to have to try to think of other places she might be. We have to use our heads on this one."

Tom walked over to Mat with a calming expression on his face. All attempts at trying to comfort the enraged teenager seemed weak and meaningless. Mat shrugged Tom's hand off his shoulder and turned to him.

"I'll tell you this much, Tom, when we do find her and that sick motherfucker, they won't be able to take him to jail. There won't be enough left of him for the police to identify. You with me on that, Tom?"

Tom dropped his brow and thought about the brutal suggestion for a minute then wholeheartedly replied, "Hell yeah, Mat. No matter what happens, that sick son of a bitch is toast if we find him."

The two young men shook hands on their deadly agreement then turned to get back into the truck. Tom stopped Mat in his tracks.

"Hey, man, let me ask you something. If you were trying to hide in this little town, where is the first place you would go?"

"Probably down to the woods or near one of the old docks on the Delaware. That's where I used to hide from the cops after curfew."

Toms face lit up.

"That's right… Now, where is the *last* place you would hide?"

Mat thought for a second.

"That's easy, somewhere in the middle of town, maybe a building on Main Street," Mat replied, wondering what Tom had up his sleeve.

Tom pointed his hand up to the small skyline of Riverside.

"Let's not forget, Mat, he's a smart sicko. He's a science teacher. So I'm sure he thought all of this out logically. If he hasn't taken her all the way to Canada by now, the most logical place to hide from people trying to find you is somewhere you can keep your eye on them, right?"

His finger pointed to the illuminated clockface of the old clock tower. The four faces of the clock glowed white, barely lighting up the night sky.

Tom continued. "I remember one time I was trying to out-run the cops. It was mischief night, and I had egged about a dozen cars. The cops chased me into Brown Street Woods and had me sur-rounded. The only thing I could think to do was climb a tree. So I got to the top of an old pine tree and waited them out. They contin-ued to look for about an hour then left. I would have left right away, but I was so high up I could see they only drove about two blocks away in each direction. If I hadn't been at the top of that tree and seen that, they would have caught me for sure. So after another hour, one of the cars left. I slipped through the opening in that direction. It's like I said, Mr. Brackstone's a smart guy."

The two boys looked at each other and smiled. They jumped into Tom's beat-up Chevy truck and raced down the nearly empty roads of Riverside, certain they knew where Colette was. Mat hopped around in his seat with an old wooden baseball bat in his hands, squeezing it tightly in anticipation of what was to come. Tom drove as fast as he could, fearing every second they wasted may be another second of torture for his longtime friend and confidant.

"Don't worry, Colette, help is on the way!" Tom said as they grew increasingly near the old abandoned clock tower, not know-ing the real and certain danger they were naively plunging them-selves into, not understanding the true evil they were about to face. Testosterone-driven, youthful bodies screaming toward unsure dan-ger through a dark and shifting night. Tragedy looming on the wind through the watchful eye of a murderous scavenger.

CHAPTER 22

Too Late

SPECIAL AGENT BRANCH ARRIVED AT Riverside High soon after he received the news of Colette's abduction. He radioed ahead for the locals to block off Mr. Brackstone's classroom. The night janitor directed Agent Branch to Mr. Brackstone's science classroom along the long, winding hallways of the run-down high school. There was already a threatening-looking local police officer stationed outside the door, waiting for Branch as he walked up.

The young, strapping deputy loomed over the classroom entrance, standing over six feet tall and weighing close to three hundred pounds. His head was shaved clean, and he sported a light-brown mustache. Every detail of his uniform fit snuggly over the large man's bulging muscles. Branch looked the bulky deputy over and approached him using his most aggressive tone.

"Deputy, has anyone of your local boys been in there fucking up my crime scene?" Branch asked in a resoundingly assertive nature.

The large man seemed shocked at the bluntness of Agent Branch's question then replied in military fashion, "No, sir, as soon as I got news you were coming, I stopped going through Mr. Brackstone's desk, just like they told me."

Branch shook his head in utter amazement.

"Okay, Barney, let's get this straight. The only thing I want you to do is stand here in front of this door. If anyone comes along that does not have FBI credentials, don't let them in. If anyone comes along that outranks you in your local jurisdiction, don't let them in. If Jesus himself comes down from heaven, wanting to walk into this classroom, don't let his ass in. Do you understand me, Barney?"

The oversize young officer looked puzzled. He first scratched his chin then replied, "Yeah, I got ya, boss. There's just one thing…"

"And what is that, Deputy?" Branch asked in rebuttal.

"My name is George, not Barney."

Branch couldn't help but blatantly laugh out loud at the naive comment.

"I'll have to make a note of that, Deputy. Now, guard this door and don't forget what I told you."

He left the confused officer in the hall and entered the room. Slipping on his surgical gloves, Branch called in for a scientific team immediately. He started looking through Mr. Brackstone's desk. There were the normal teaching tools in most of the drawers: graded papers, markers, scientific textbooks, and old handouts. Looking through the room was going to be an all-night affair. Branch took his jacket off and settled in for the long haul.

He noticed after a while how clinical Mr. Brackstone kept his classroom. There was no personality to the room. The papers were graded with only numbers, no comments on performance. Mr. Brackstone's desk was exceedingly hygienic, sterile even. Branch devised how methodical this man was. Everything in its place, nothing that would arouse suspicion. He could not understand how a man that seemed so logical on paper could do the things he was now being accused.

Branch came to the bottom of one of the drawers and noticed a small journal that had a cheap lock on it. Branch easily picked the lock and opened the small black book with resounding curiosity. The first page was covered with poorly drawn pentagrams, followed by several more pages of the same. The only text that appeared in the book was a lone poem written by Mr. Brackstone himself, dated just two days prior. It read:

If you could think or feel the reproach of this man,
Reach out softly, touch his hand.
This man would become flesh to you.
Not a figure of stone, to be looked through.
Genuine blood, who feels the stairs,
Hears the whispers,
Fears the glares,
His voice that echoes
No one hears.
A gossip point to all his peers.
Young ones laugh,
Mock his life.
He will deliver them with avenging strife.
He speaks empty echoes,
Wanders alone.
The true beast inside,
A chill to the bone.

Signed,
Mr. Cliff Brackstone

Branch slowly closed the bizarre hardback journal. He now thought of Mr. Brackstone as a man torn between two very different mentalities: one being a creature seeking some sort of social acceptance, and the other, horribly striking out at society for what he was. Branch had no doubt in his mind of Mr. Brackstone's complete guilt. Through many years of federal service, Agent Branch had seen many documents and social profiles on serial killers. He knew all too well what to look for, and Mr. Brackstone fit the bill perfectly. Branch scratched his head and questioned himself.

"If Mildred is right about you, and I pray to God she isn't, you have been a very busy man, Mr. Brackstone. Just how busy is the question I need answered. Let's just hope you left enough clues around here for me to pick up your sour scent."

The mentally tired field agent bagged the black journal as evidence. The scientific team arrived from the Philadelphia office moments later. Branch recognized the old scientist heading up the team of insecure bookworms. Tyler Lundy was one of the oldest and most respected CSI crime scene investigators in the FBI. He had been a key member in several high-profile investigations throughout his career. Tyler stood only five feet tall but weighed at least as much as Branch. He waddled forward, looking over his thick-rimmed glasses with his hands in his pockets and inspecting the room as he entered.

"Good to see they sent you in on this one, Tyler," Branch exclaimed as he shook the old man's portly hand.

"Ah, Special Agent Branch. Good to see you again, son. I have been given the basics on the case over the wire. What I need from you on this case is very simple."

"And what would that be, sir?"

"Get these local yokels away from my fucking crime scene as soon as possible."

Branch smiled from ear to ear.

"Finally, a man that hears what I'm saying. It's already been taken care of, sir. Hey, it looks like those Philly cheesesteaks are treating you pretty good over in the city office."

Tyler patted his belly and laughed.

"You know, being assigned to the fattest city in America was the worst thing that could have happened to my gut. Mrs. Lundy doesn't complain, though. You know what they say: the heavier the hammer, the harder you can pound the nail."

Branch vigorously laughed out loud at the crude yet hysterical comment.

The old man let out a jolly giggle then continued. "Good, then we can get started. After we bag some of the usual things, I have a new toy I would like to use on this one, Branch, with your permission, of course."

Branch scowled at the old wiseass.

"Permission granted, old wise and wonderful wizard of CSI. Now, what kind of toy are we talking about?"

"Oh, it is a wonderful invention. It's been around for a while, but the boys in Washington just got around to funding it last year. First, I have to dust the room with a special synthetic chemical that bonds with remnants of human blood or DNA. Then, using a very expensive tax-dollar-paid lamp, we can see what our boy has been up to around here. The more recent the genetic material, the better the results will be. So, time is a factor, Branch."

"Sounds good to me, Tyler. I'll get out of your way and let your team go to work. I'm going to run down to the main office and see if I can dig anything up on Mr. Brackstone and his next of kin. Let me know when you have something from your new federally funded toy, Tyler."

"You got it, Branch."

The old portly man began to order his meandering team of scientists around immediately. Branch exited the room and instructed Deputy George to lead him to the main office. After a couple of twists and turns down the main hallway, they came to the office. Branch quickly found the personal files of the teachers and flipped through it until he came to Mr. Brackstone's thin file. The description was one of a textbook teacher. He marked high on his administrative observations and seemed to be a model teacher as far as the schoolboard was concerned.

Unfortunately for Agent Branch, there were no contact numbers on his personal information sheet in case of an emergency. He called all the information into headquarters. Only seconds later, they came back with intel. His father was still listed under his medical history. And he was still alive. Branch jotted down the name and address in his case file with a question mark at the end of it. The sound of Darth Vader's intro music from the *Star Wars* movies started playing loudly over Branch's cell phone.

"Special Agent Branch here."

"Agent Branch, it's Tyler. You need to get up here right away. There's a situation here."

"On my way!" Branch shouted, already running through the main office door. Deputy George followed in stride, asking what was going on. Branch had no time to stop and coddle the confused deputy, though he would have loved to give him some more shit.

Rounding the corridor to Mr. Brackstone's classroom, he noticed all the scientists from Tyler's team were outside in the hallway. One of the younger scientists in Tyler's squad was bent over a trash can in the process of vomiting. Even Tyler Lundy, a seasoned veteran of CSI, looked shaken up as sweat poured down his wrinkled brow. Branch composed himself and approached Tyler with a questioning look.

"What the hell did you find in there Tyler?"

"It's like nothing I ever imagined, I just can't believe it. It's so horrible."

"Tyler, what are you talking about? Just catch your breath and try to explain yourself."

"We have a devil on our hands, Branch. A devil like I've never seen."

Tyler motioned for him to go into the classroom. Branch had never seen Tyler like this. His face was pale white, and he was bent over in confused disbelief. Branch entered the room cautiously, witnessing what made his comrades disperse into the hallway. The special florescent floodlights loomed ominously overhead. They rested on large industrial tripods illuminating the dark classroom in a gray speckled haze. The chemical agent that bonded with the blood and DNA residue illuminated the room in fluorescent green light. The classroom was painted in pain, covered in neon-green drag marks, handprints, and what looked like puddles. There was a section of the back wall that brandished the green outline of someone's face that had been smashed into the harsh, cold cinder block repeatedly. It was so detailed even the shape of small neon-green teeth on the suffering face seemed to scream out in pain. The sheer horror of the scene would haunt Agent Branch and all who witnessed it for the rest of their lives.

Branch reluctantly pushed on and rounded the back entrance to the rear storage room. So much neon green illuminated in the small room that it lit up Branch's face and clothing, forcing him to cover his stunned eyes for a moment. On the back wall of the room, there was a message that traumatized Branch and sent a bizarre chill through his trembling body. Spelled out in illuminated neon green were the striking words *too late.*

CHAPTER 23

Rats in a Cage

A DULL, REPETITIVE SOUND OF monotonous cricket songs pierced the stale night's silence. Tom cautiously inched his rusty truck up to the back fence of the old clock tower complex. Only the locals knew of the back entrance to the abandoned building. The two would-be heroes leaped out of the car, Mat brandishing his wooden bat and Tom holding a heavy metal tire iron poised to strike. The noisy crickets deadened as they approached the tall grass in front of an iron fence. Throwing the weapons over the fence, the boys vehemently climbed the noisy chain links up and over the top. Enough noise rattled off the rusty links to arouse barking from the local junkyard dog just across the street. They had just surely ruined any chance of a stealthy entrance into the building.

The back door was made of solid, reinforced steel. Unfortunately for them, it was locked from the inside. They just had to find another way in. Tom scouted around and found a nearby basement window. Luckily, the basement window grating was missing. The hasty investigators quickly squeezed themselves through the tiny opening. Once they managed to force their way in, they quickly noticed the pitch-black basement was without any light source.

"Did you bring a flashlight?" Tom asked as he fumbled around in the dark.

"I knew we forgot something," Mat replied while trying to feel his way around like a blind man in a strange home. Suddenly, they both heard a peculiar noise in the corner of the room. Then, another from the next room over. Fear embezzled its ugly head into the heroic hearts of the noble do-gooders.

"Did you hear that, Tom? Sounds like someone is in here with us…"

"Don't be stupid, Mat. It's pitch-black in here. It's got to be a rat or a cat or something like that," Tom replied in a pissy tone.

"Oh, okay, genius. Or maybe it could be a hat or a bat or a fat retarded vat of spat."

"You can be such a dickhead, dude. Let's just find some light so we can find out if Colette is even here. You remember her, right? Your girlfriend? The reason we are in this dark, dingy, stinky basement searching around like a couple of dopes?"

The mention of his girlfriend's name brought Mat back to his senses. This was no time to goof around.

"You're right, man, my bad. We got a job to do, so let's take care of this sick bastard and find my lady."

"That's the spirit, soldier. Let's get down to some serious search and destroy."

The two determined youths continued to feel their way through the dark lower level of the clock tower, hopelessly fumbling around through dusty old furniture and boxes. The stench of rotting cardboard filled the moldy basement, making the air almost unfit to be breathed. Tom couldn't walk half an inch without having to fight through another set of double-layered cobwebs or dust bunnies. Finally, they came to a hallway where a dim light from an outside window gave them some idea of where they were.

"Hey, Mat, I think that must be the service elevator to the top of the tower at the end of the hall."

"Yeah, good call, dude. Let's see if we can hitch a ride on that thing, if it still works, that is."

The newly invigorated boys continued down the dark hallway. Another disheartening sound came barreling into their eardrums from the end of the dark corridor. This time, the boys didn't say a word to each other. No cat or rodent could make that kind of noise. A sullen terror left a rancid taste lingering in the musty air. They nervously gripped their weapons tight and proceeded to tiptoe toward the old steel doors of the service lift. The doors were stuck open in the elevator entrance, revealing the empty shaft bottom through the archway. In the shaft, they found an old wooden ladder visibly leading up to what looked like the ground floor.

"What do you think, Tom? Should we try another way or go up this crusty-looking thing?" Mat asked in no more than a whisper.

"Hell, I don't know, man. It's up to you. I got your back no matter what. So it's your call if you wanna give it a go," Tom replied in his own hushed tone. With the gentleness of a lamb, the two boys guardedly entered the elevator shaft and began to ascend the old wooden rungs of the dusty ladder. As Mat neared the top of the ladder, he heard a slow grinding noise from underneath him. The old elevator doors from the basement entrance were closing.

"Tom, what's going on down there?"

"I don't know. The doors just closed underneath us. Hurry up and get up the ladder!" Tom said with a penetrating fear in his voice.

Mat scurried up the ancient climbing device frantically. The opening to the next level was a mere three steps away. Then, without warning, over the top of the ladder, Mat beheld the unwelcome white, mealy face of Mr. Cliff Brackstone. He revealed his yellow teeth, wickedly smiling at the athletic star, subsequently pushing the top of the ladder into the opposite wall of the shaft. Both boys fell to the bottom of the elevator passage and slammed into the unforgiving concrete floor.

Tom heard a disgusting crack and sat up to see his left leg turned backward in the opposite direction of his knee. A jagged ivory bone protruded from his leg, ripping out the side of his jeans. The severely injured youth screamed in agony. Mat landed flat on his back, slamming his head into the remorseless concrete floor of the elevator shaft. When Mat regained his wits, his eyes grew wide as he saw the horrendous condition of his friend. Mat immediately forced the ladder back toward the opening and started to climb it once again. Unfortunately for him, Mr. Brackstone was still perched at the top of the shaft, waiting for one of them to push the ladder back to him.

Mr. Brackstone quickly saturated the top three rungs of the ladder with lighter fluid and struck a match. The top of the old wooden ladder ignited in flames in a matter of seconds. Mat caught a face full of fire and once again fell violently ten feet to the bottom of the shaft, this time landing on top of his already-handicapped friend's protruding leg bone. Another nasty crunch echoed through the shaft as Tom's exposed bone smacked off the stone floor. They both bellowed out in unbearable pain as pieces of the ladder rained fiery debris on top of them. Mr. Brackstone gloated at his handiwork from his perched position. The maniacal killer watched with profound elation as the two boys dodged and scurried away from the fiery remnants of the ladder. Once the lighter fluid burned off, the ladder stopped burning and smoldered black soot filtered down on the teenagers' writhing bodies. Two fallen heroes lay at the bottom of the elevator shaft, broken and defeated. Mr. Brackstone leaned over the shaft, hocked up his entire throat, and spit at the boys.

He gleefully exclaimed, "Once again, the power of the mind overcomes the power of the body. Darwin's chain remains strong. I am the strong, and you are the weak. I grow more powerful with every one of you little bastards I wipe off the face of the earth. I hope you boys are proud of your efforts. You stumbled right into my trap. Now, you're mine!"

Mat wiped the sloppy remnants of ash and spit from his beaten face. Tears streamed down the once-proud athlete's cheeks as he screamed up the dark passage in anger.

"You sick motherfucker! What kind of a man are you? You are nothing! If you were to come down here, I would rip your fucking head off!"

Mr. Brackstone laughed at the enraged youth's bold comments.

"Well, that may be true in theory, Mat, but with me up here and you down there, I believe I have the upper hand. Oh, and those doors behind you are solid steel, so I wouldn't waste my time trying to open them. The only way to do that is with the rewired control panel that I have up here with me. You know, I really should be proud of myself. A couple of my students figured out where I was before the cops. I must have taught you something deduction well, huh, boys? Well, that's enough chitchat for now. I have to go ditch your truck before daylight. I don't want any other uninvited guests snooping around here. Oh, just one more thing, Mat... Colette is a real wildcat, if you know what I mean."

Mat screamed frantically, "Fuck you, you sick son of a bitch! Fuck you! I'm going to kill you!"

As the doors to the first floor slammed shut behind Mr. Brackstone, the boys were left in total darkness. Tom whimpered in pain and gathered himself up into a fetal position. Mat sat down in shock.

He looked to Tom and asked, "How could such a small, worthless human being like Mr. Brackstone have done all of this?"

Tom looked up with tears in his eyes and answered, "Because we underestimated him, Mat. Now, we are going to die a cruel death for our foolish arrogance."

"That's not true, Tom. Don't say shit like that. That's what quitters say before they lose. You don't know this is the end. We can make it out of here alive. We just have to use our heads."

"Okay, Mat. Then why don't you use your head and think of something? I have a bloody bone sticking out of my fucking leg, man. Do you see that sick shit? I am bleeding like a stuck pig all over the bottom of this dirty, rat-infested elevator shaft. I am going to fucking die if you don't get me out of here soon. Let's face it, we messed up really bad on this one. We should have called the cops like I thought of doing, not tried to play the hero."

Mat turned away from his tortured partner and gathered his knees up to his chest. The once-proud macho athlete proceeded to openly cry. Sad sounds of human suffering bellowed through the gloomy passage. The only discernable echoes were those of his whimpering tears and Tom's somber moans of pain.

CHAPTER 24

The Visit

THE FOLLOWING MORNING'S NEWS CARRIED quickly through Riverside and chilled the microscopic town like a cold breeze running down a wet back. Mildred awoke inhospitably to a thundering knock at her cheap motel door. She sat up begrudgingly, still dressed in her clothes from the day before. Dragging herself out of bed, the half-alive agent unhappily answered the door. Agent Branch stood in the doorway looking as clean and well-dressed as ever. He smiled at the disheveled agent and handed her a large cup of piping hot coffee. Mildred took a full gulp, put on her sunglasses, and headed out into the parking lot. Branch stopped her before she got into his spotless car to inquire about the next move.

"Mildred, I was looking through Mr. Brackstone's files last night and saw that his father is still alive. I think we should check him out. He may have some possible leads for us."

"Sounds like a good call, Branch. Let me call in the name, and we'll get any priors on him."

Mildred paused for a second then continued, "Look, Branch, I know I dropped the ball on this one. You could have dropped me from this case the second you got here. I just want you to know I appreciate you keeping me on, and I won't slip up again."

Branch looked compassionately into Mildred's eyes and gave her a cool, accepting wink. Mildred nodded and radioed in for the information as she slid into the car. Branch sat down in the driver's seat next to her. He carefully looked at Mildred then began his inspirational speech.

"Look here, girl. There isn't anything you can do about what's happened so far. You can't go back in time and make it all better. You have to stay cool. Think about what we can do to catch this maniac. We are going to have to outsmart this one. From what I've seen, it's going to take both of us to do it. So stop feeling sorry for yourself and get on the job, Agent. Got it?"

"I got it, Branch. As long as you're sure you want me on this case?"

With a shocked look on his face, Branch confidently replied, "Am I sure I want you on this case? Shit, give me a pissed-off white girl with a personal vendetta and a gun on every case, and they're going to start calling me Elliot fuckin' Ness."

The two laughed off the joke as if they were lifelong friends. An awkward pause ensued after the laughter died down. Mildred's hungry eyes invited Branch's masculine instincts. They obviously looked each other up and down but were soon sidetracked by the information they were waiting for. It quickly came in over the wire. The muffled voice of the dispatcher began.

"The books have several prior arrests on your call-in. He was arrested or detained at least five times for domestics. It looks like he was a wife beater. There are a couple of tickets after that, but he hasn't done anything in the last twenty years on the books."

Branch pulled out of the parking lot and raced down the road toward the Whiteside Funeral Home. It was the last known address of Mr. Brackstone's father. When they pulled up to the morbid manor, a funeral was in session. Agent Branch lowered his head to pay his respects to the recently departed. Mildred hid behind him carefully in fear she might notice a familiar face. They waited patiently outside the funeral parlor for the quiet group of mourners to file out.

Branch asked the funeral director if he knew where they could find Mr. Brackstone's father. The serious man led them into the back room of the building. The director looked over his shoulder and placed a hushing look on his face.

"Please try to respect the recently passed and keep the noise down in here. We have other mourners outside."

Branch replied, "Sure thing, sir. I assure you, we only have a few questions and will be on our way."

He led the determined duo into the cold dressing room full of dead bodies. Mr. Brackstone's ancient father seemed hard at work, bent over a fresh corpse. He was in the process of injecting embalming fluid into the unfortunate, lifeless body that lay sprawled out on the shiny metal table.

"Mr. Brackstone, I am Special Agent Branch from the FBI. I need to ask you some questions about your son, Mr. Cliff Brackstone. Is there somewhere we can go to discuss this?"

The elderly man barely moved in recognition of the request. While continuing his morbid work, he replied in an accusing tone, "I have a ton of work to do, fella. Anything you want to ask me, I can answer from here."

Looking a bit bewildered, Branch began his interview.

"Mr. Brackstone, we would like to know when was the last time you saw or spoke with your son?"

The elderly man continued his morbid work, jamming a long fixed metal plunger into the stagnant corpse's bloated abdomen. It made a disgusting crunch as it entered the lifeless body. The old mortician twisted the cold device back and forth, forcing it through the ridged rigor mortis—riddled abdominal muscles of the deceased man. Without breaking stride in his work, Mr. Brackstone's father replied hesitantly, "I haven't seen that boy in a long time. I don't really have any care to ever see him again. He's rotten to the core, and I'm sure that's the reason you folks are here bothering me. I'm sure he's done something terrible."

"What would make you say that, Mr. Brackstone?" Branch asked in high anticipation.

The old man angrily looked up from his tedious work. His face was weathered and colorless. A heavy gray film of cataracts covered his eyes. He felt his way over to the control panel of the embalming machine. As he flicked a large red switch, the machine began to hum, and a clean line of formaldehyde flowed into the corpse. Another line of pure red blood flowed into a bucket on the floor. The half-blind man worked his way toward the agents, wiping his hands clean with a dirty rag. He paused for a second, and then replied, "Oh, I see, you have come here for the story. You want to know what made him the way he is."

Branch rudely interrupted, "What way is that, sir?"

"I'm just an old man, so don't interrupt me when I'm talking, I lose my train of thought too easily. Well, take a seat, and I'll tell you his story then. Just don't expect there to be any happy endings. Back when I was a teenager, my father sent me to work here at the Whiteside Funeral Home. He said it was a good job, something that would never go out of style. I worked on the dead bodies morning, noon, and night. To say the least, it dulled my senses a bit. I thought I would be alone forever until the day Mr. Whiteside's daughter came back from boarding school. She was the light in my life from the moment I laid eyes on her. Well, it wasn't too long after that we got married. The first year of our marriage was incredible. We were so happy back then…"

Mr. Brackstone's father wiped fresh tears from his wrinkled face and continued.

"That is, we were happy until she got pregnant. When she was going through the pregnancy, her entire personality changed. She went from easygoing to high-strung in a matter of weeks. As she got further along, her attitude grew worse. I don't know if it was the thought of rearing her own child or having to grow up too fast, but whatever it was, she had changed for the worse.

"In her ninth month, there was an accident. We had an argument, and somehow she fell down the staircase. I don't remember too well these days. I rushed her to the hospital, and that's when Mr. Brackstone's sorry ass was brought into the world. The fall had injured my wife severely. The doctors did the best they could patching her up, but she wound up having a large permanent hump on her back thanks to the fall. In her mind, she changed forever, from a pretty young woman into a deformed freak. I never saw her like that. After she got home, she wouldn't even look at Mr. Brackstone. As ridiculous as it sounds, I think she blamed him for what happened.

I didn't know much about bringing up a child. I did a poor job. Mr. Brackstone grew up unloved by his mother. She turned even sourer as Mr. Brackstone grew older. Her entire personality became tainted, she transformed into an evil person. She became abusive with me, so I up and left her. I just couldn't take living in the same house with that kind of a person. I should have taken the boy with me. But I left him there, all alone, with her."

The old man put his hands on his forehead and seemed to daze off in a daydream of self-pity.

"Mr. Brackstone, what happened after you left?" Mildred asked in a forgiving tone.

Gathering his composure, the half-senile man continued. "Oh, yes. Then, I hardly ever saw the boy. His mother kept him under lock and key. She told me I was no good and had no right to see him. I didn't know what was going on in that house altogether, but I know she abused that boy."

"How do you know that, sir?" Mildred said, interrupting the old man's grave story.

"Well, I know that by the way his mother died. You see, Mr. Brackstone's dog ripped her to shreds. Dogs just don't go around killing people every day for no good reason. I met Mr. Brackstone's dog a couple times. That dog was as friendly and loyal as they come. Nope, she must have been beating him pretty good that night, and I imagine that wasn't the only time either."

The two FBI agents looked at each other, and then Branch asked, "Speaking of beatings, we have your name in our files for domestic abuse on your wife on several occasions, Mr. Brackstone. What can you tell us about that?"

The old man sighed.

"You want to know if I put my hands on the boy? No! Now his mother was a different story. I would see the bruises on my boy, and I lost it a couple of times. She deserved it. It was different back then. You took care of those things in the family."

Mildred tried to shift the conversation back to Mr. Brackstone.

"What happened after that, Mr. Brackstone?"

The old man made his way over to the full bucket of blood set up underneath the corpse. He carried it over to the sink, pouring out the sickening contents at a drab pace. The old man was noticeably upset by the questioning but steadily continued his story.

"Then the boy came to live with me. He had changed though. He really wasn't a boy anymore. It's like he had seen too much. I've never seen a boy that young with so much cold hatred in his eyes. I let him do whatever he wanted. Tell you the truth, I was scared to tell him otherwise. He seemed to do well in school, so when the time came, he commuted over to the State University in Camden and picked up his teaching degree. I haven't heard from him in a long time now. I knew this day would come though. I just wish things worked out different, that's all."

Mildred was surprised by the openness of the old man. Her instincts told her to feel pity, but her hatred for Mr. Brackstone would not allow that. Instead, she felt sincerely sorry for the old man and his fallen dreams. She walked over to him and implored. "Mr. Brackstone, is there anything you can tell us that will help us find your son? So that we can put a stop to all the pain and suffering?"

The old man turned away from Mildred, took a long deep breath, visibly upset by her invasive personal question, and stated, "Pain and suffering. What do you know about any of that? How dare you refer to the capture of my boy as an end to pain and suffering! What pain are you referring to, Agent?"

"I just meant I wanted to see an end to all of the hurt this town has seen. You need to accept that it is your boy who caused this mess and help us out."

"I don't have to do anything, you bitch. He's my boy no matter what he's done. You think I would just turn him over to you government scumbags? I'm not afraid of you, I'm too old. You can't do anything to me I would care about. All of that was done a long time ago."

Branch stepped in front of Mildred. He bellied up to the old mortician and imposed his will without question.

"Now listen, sir, we are here trying to bring an end to this. You don't want to help us, that's your business. All's you are going to do is fail your son again."

The old man sank back inside himself. He curled his arms across his chest and dropped his head down in defiance of Branch's request. He only let out a crotchety humph in reply. Mildred tried to push past Branch to continue her line of questioning, but he held her back and started to head for the front exit.

Before exiting the somber room, Agent Branch turned back and relayed, "You know we are going to get him with or without your help. You do know that, right?"

The callous mortician glared at Branch through grayish-hazed orbs. A slight glimmer of his black pupil seemed to emerge and look sharply into the agent's eyes. Then to the surprise of Branch, the mortician smiled at him. Not just any smile. It was the smile of a madman. Branch had only seen it a couple of times before in his career, but always from between the bars at the federal prison for the criminally insane. The look scared the seasoned veteran. Not the kind of scare you get from a cheesy horror movie. It truly scared him, like the first time you really know you are about to get into a car accident and there is nothing you can do to stop it. The crazed mortician implied a warning to them.

"Don't think for a second that I am rooting for his capture. I don't know everything that he's done or is going to do. But I know he is severe. The most formidable man you will ever hunt. I wish you no luck. I hope you fail. If you come up against my boy, I hope with all of my black heart that he comes out on top. I can't help you, I won't help you. I don't know where he is, but I will tell you this: when you find my son, be wary. The devil himself resides in that boy."

CHAPTER 25

Morning Light

MR. CLIFF BRACKSTONE SAT MOTIONLESS on the sand-covered bank of the Delaware River. Nature surrounded his strange aura, and he felt at ease with himself. He embraced the morning light as if it were nourishment to his soul, heavily breathing in the cool, fresh air, carefree to what events were transpiring in the world around him. Mr. Brackstone walked the muddy shoreline leisurely, taking in the daybreak radiance. He wondered how such a wonderful sight could be overlooked by so many people every day. As he neared a small detachable steel bridge that linked Riverside with its neighboring town of Delanco, he peered out at the shadows of the willows dancing on the shoreline. They mesmerized the slight man. The shadows appeared to claw at the sand and mud of the shoreline, never making a scratch.

A sharp noise quickly snapped Mr. Brackstone out of his daze. Mr. Brackstone looked auspiciously up to the Gothic clock tower. The bells in the tower chimed seven times, and the old factory whistle blew abruptly, echoing down the empty streets, calling to the ghosts of long-dead watch-factory workers. Mr. Brackstone sat beside the bridge. He opened his briefcase and ate some delicious golden apples he had tucked away for just such an occasion. The warm beams of sunlight danced over the now-calm river, illuminating the seldom-seen bottom of the historical body of water.

Mr. Brackstone noticed something shining at the bottom of the river. It seemed as if a flashlight was at the murky bottom pointing up at him. He cautiously inched closer to the water's edge like a mouse looking out of his den for predators. The sun revealed itself farther into the morning sky. Mr. Brackstone began to make out the object stuck at the bottom of the river. It wasn't glass or metal as he had imagined. The light was coming from a pair of glowing cat eyes, staring at Mr. Brackstone from the murky waters below. Mr. Brackstone backed away quickly from the shore and caught his breath.

"Surely it is something else," he said to himself in doubt.

He reapproached the muddy bank of the river. Mr. Brackstone looked again into the water. The same glowing eyes shone toward him. This time, the impending glare of doom rose closer to the surface, climbing from the depths of the Delaware at a cumbersome pace. Mr. Brackstone cleaned off his spectacles with his shirttail and could finally make out the decomposed face of one of his lifeless victims. The ghastly form floated up to the surface, eyes shining as if powered by the sun. Moss and algae dripped off the greenish living corpse as it emerged from its watery grave.

Mr. Brackstone fell back on the muddy bank in disbelief. The decomposing zombie emerged from the water, dragging its mangled feet through the mud and sand of the small shore embankment. Green chunks of flesh hung from its decrepit face. Earthworms squirmed through gaping holes in its neck and chest. A small perch fluttered through a gaping hole in the monster's stomach and bounced itself back into the water. Mr. Brackstone toiled to get back to his feet. With surprising speed, the zombie leaped at Mr. Brackstone's legs. It grabbed hold of one of his legs and locked its rotting teeth onto Mr. Brackstone's ankle.

"No!" Mr. Brackstone screamed like a shocked schoolgirl receiving her first inappropriate touch.

He jerked his stringy leg free of the heinous beast then ran down the bank, fighting his way through the tall grass and mud, checking behind him to see how close the creature was following. The slight zombie lumbered after Mr. Brackstone, making an awful moaning sound, like the one old people make in the dentist chair. Mr. Brackstone tripped over a large piece of driftwood on the river-bank. His face slammed into the mud, cracking his glasses in two and opening a small wound just over his left eyebrow. Once again, he got up to his feet, this time brandishing a large branch to defend himself. A small stream of fresh crimson blood began to drip from his wound, steadily over his glasses and down his face. The horrid zombie grew closer to Mr. Brackstone.

He cried out, "I killed you! You're dead, this is impossible!"

The monster made no attempt to rebut his claim but stopped in its tracks. Then, with the grotesque gaze of a troll, she pointed past Mr. Brackstone and smiled. Earthworms and maggots poured out of the zombie's mouth as its bottom jaw dropped to the ground, digging itself into the sand. Mr. Brackstone immediately held his mouth. The normally cold-blooded killer, finally finding his line of discomfort, swallowed back the vomit that had been forcing its way up his throat. He turned on his heels to run like a coward, then witnessed what the delighted zombie was smiling about.

Surrounding him, on the bank of the Delaware, there were eighteen of the most grotesquely dismembered corpses ever to be seen on earth. All his victims he had submerged into the depths of the gloomy Delaware stood reanimated in front of him—some, missing limbs; others, missing heads. One of them even stood backward to Mr. Brackstone because its head was turned one hundred and eighty degrees the wrong way. All with eyes burning brighter than the heart of a raging inferno in Mr. Brackstone's direction.

Mr. Brackstone swung the branch he'd been dragging with him wildly in self-defense. The zombies closed in on him. Their decomposing hands worked to overpower the weak man. He swung his medieval club at the largest one's head, summarily removing it from its body. The creature reached down with one hand and snatched its head off the sand then firmly reattached it. Mr. Brackstone screamed like a small child as the zombies ripped and tore at his soft flesh. The large zombie he had struck dug its lifeless teeth into Mr. Brackstone's ear and ripped it off amid a red haze spaying across its green face. He tried to scurry underneath them in a last desperate means of escape. One by one, the monstrous creatures dug their rotting teeth into Mr. Brackstone's body, tearing living chunks of bloody flesh from his tortured remains. He pleaded for help from anywhere.

"Oh my god… Please stop! I am sorry for what I did. Please stop eating me!"

The undead creatures clamped onto Mr. Brackstone's legs and dragged him, crying and screaming into the depths of the Delaware River. As he desperately gulped for his last breath of air, Mr. Brackstone woke up in a puddle of his own sweat.

"It was all a dream," Mr. Brackstone said to himself in relief.

He looked at his cheap watch and rolled out of bed.

"Time to take care of some more projects," he said as he dressed himself in a Domino's pizza uniform.

CHAPTER 26

Deal with the Devil

COLETTE LOOKED AROUND THE SMALL room that entrapped her. She tugged at her restraints in disgust. Her energy was almost fully drained. She could barely keep her bloodshot eyes open for longer than a couple of minutes at a time. The thought of Mr. Brackstone viciously taking her kept her awake throughout the night. Bubbling in her stomach constantly reminded her of how bad she had to use the bathroom. Her own putrid waste endlessly tortured her, rolling and churning around in her bowels. She closed her legs together tightly and tried to keep her mind on something else though she knew she was fighting a losing battle with herself and, eventually, her will would give in to the primal calls of her digestive system's accursed request.

Mr. Brackstone left a gallon of crystal clear water on the other side of the room, well out of her reach. Hungrily looking at the water so close, yet so far, was worse than the pains in her stomach. She stared at the translucent liquid like a wild animal, licking her powder-dry lips to no avail.

The small trapdoor in the far corner of the room creaked open. Mr. Brackstone climbed up into the room sometime after twelve in the afternoon. Colette knew the time by the number of rings from the neighboring bells. They chimed so loud the entire room vibrated and shook. Mr. Brackstone walked over to his cot and flopped down in joyful exhaustion.

Colette inspected her capturer. It looked as though he had been running a marathon. He was drenched with sweat and couldn't catch his breath, even after resting in the bed for five minutes. Though she was almost positive he was too tired to try anything, Colette clenched her fists in anticipation of another attack. She held her defensive stance for about ten minutes until she realized Mr. Brackstone was really much too exhausted to even sit up.

"You should have seen it, Colette. It was wonderful," Mr. Brackstone bragged as he turned to look at his dehydrated hostage.

"Seen what, you sick bastard?" replied Colette in a catty tone.

"Well, aren't we the trash mouth? I wouldn't have expected that from you, young lady. You really should try to be on your best behavior. It won't be long until you're completely out of energy. Then, you will be at my mercy. And good manners might do you well." Mr. Brackstone paused. "Anyway, to answer your rude question, the wonderful thing you missed. Well. Let's just say, a couple of your friends figured out our private location and tried to crash our little party. I think you know Tom and Mat, don't you?" Mr. Brackstone sneered at the tired youth and let out an evil giggle.

"Oh no... What do you mean? What are you talking about? You didn't hurt them, did you? If you hurt them, I swear to God I'll—"

Mr. Brackstone abruptly interrupted, "You'll do what? You are in no position to do anything, Colette. In fact, I'm sure you are barely able to hold your own bowels right now, let alone break free of your ropes and attack me. You have a lot of courage, Colette, but that isn't going to win you any awards with me. Like I told you before, soon you will be at my mercy. Now sit there and shut that pretty little mouth so I can tell you what your friends' sticky situation is."

Colette slumped back against the ridged wall. She stared at Mr. Brackstone with a newfound hatred and rose up her right hand. One by one, she curled back her fingers until only the middle one remained.

"Here's a sticky situation for you," she replied in rebellion to Mr. Brackstone's pompous order.

Mr. Brackstone only smiled at her. He swung his legs out over the cot and sat on the edge of the bed.

"All right, tough girl, let's see if your condescending attitude changes after I tell you this. Your football-hero boyfriend and his auto-shop buddy found our hiding place. I don't know how they figured it out. Though I can tell you they weren't smart enough to tell anyone else. Otherwise, you might have been rescued by now. Ah, the pure stupidity of teenagers. It's a wonderful thing. Well, like I was saying. They found us last night. I watched them barrel down the road to get here. They gave me plenty of time to spring my little trap on them. I even got stuck in the same room down in the basement with them, and they *still* couldn't catch me. I guess they should have brought a flashlight, huh? Well, I'm sure you can figure out the rest. I out-smarted them, and now they lay at the bottom of the service elevator shaft at my mercy. I don't know if I will kill them right away or make them suffer a bit. What do you think about that, my defiant princess?"

Colette stood up and tugged against her ropes, blaring out an emotional response, "You're full of shit! You don't have them. You're just trying to make me give in. I don't believe you."

Mr. Brackstone reached into his bag and pulled out a video camera.

"You need some unadulterated verification then? I will be back shortly, Colette, and then we can discuss this further."

Mr. Brackstone gladly left the room. He happily prepared his video camera to record as he neared the second-floor elevator doors, which he had hot-wired shut. He could hear faint screams for help echoing through the dark shaft. Mr. Brackstone put his ear to the door to listen for a while, giggling with delight at the sheer terror he had created, before he bothered the two desperate boys.

"Help! Somebody help us!" Mat screamed into the empty dark-ness of the lifeless tunnel.

His voice was hoarse and almost gone. He had been screaming all night, hoping someone might hear his plea for help and come to rescue them. Tom had passed out earlier in the night from pain and blood loss. Mat fashioned a makeshift splint over his friend's broken leg with his belt and some old wooden planks from the bottom of the shaft, but the bleeding still hadn't stopped by morning. Mat pounded at the metal doors all night long until his hands were bloody. He finally gave up when his wooden bat cracked into pieces against the harsh juggernaut.

The second-floor doors opened slowly, revealing the first light Mat had seen since he and his foolish partner were trapped by Mr. Brackstone the night before. He covered his eyes and screamed up the shaft, hoping someone had found them.

"Help! We're down here! Hey, look down here, my friend is hurt, and we need a doctor. Help!"

"Oh, I'm not here to help you, Mat. I just wanted to get some pictures for your girlfriend. You see, she called me a liar upstairs, so I need a little proof that her big brawny football player and her half-dead friend are really trapped like two rats in a cage."

"You touch one hair on her head, and I'll kill you. Did you hear me, Brackstone? I'll kill you!" Mat screamed at the top of his raspy voice.

"Wow, you must really be on the same wavelength with Colette. She just said the same thing to me." Mr. Brackstone laughed as he clicked on the miniature spotlight that was mounted to his video camera.

"Now, say something nice to your lady friend. I'm sure she would love to hear how much you love her or some crap like that."

Mat looked up at the light. He realized this might be the last chance he ever had to say something to his high school love. He tearfully began a heartfelt speech.

"Colette, I love you, baby. Don't give in. I don't care what that sick fucker tells you, he isn't going to let us go. Fight as long as you can. Fight with everything you have, baby. The whole town is looking for you. Just remember, whatever happens, I will never stop loving you."

Mat fell to his knees and sobbed openly for Mr. Brackstone's camera. Mr. Brackstone turned the spotlight off and clapped.

"Very emotional, Mat. I didn't know you had a soft side to you. Well, I'm sure she will love your speech. I'll play it for her right before I have my way with her. How does that sound?"

Mr. Brackstone sealed the second-floor doors behind him. The total absence of light fell back onto the two would-be heroes, leaving the boys at the bottom of the elevator shaft looking up into darkness once again. Tom had woken up during the conversation.

He turned to look at Mat and asked, "What are we going to do now, Mat?"

Mat looked at his friend with swollen eyes and replied, "Pray, Tom, because God is the only one that can help our sorry asses now."

Mr. Brackstone scurried back up to the top floor in eager anticipation of Colette's reaction. He swiftly emerged through the trapdoor, only to be greeted in utter filth. Colette pelted her skinny abductor with handfuls of her own excrement. The first shit ball hit Mr. Brackstone in the side of the face, sticking to his pasty, white skin like superglue. The second one hit unswervingly across his chest, covering his shirt in a brownish-green splash. The horrid smell of human waste was overwhelming. Mr. Brackstone fell down the short wooden ladder leading up to the room and crashed down onto the solid floor. He could feel his already-swollen ribs throbbing in pain. Bit by bit, he wiped Colette's rancid-smelling shit from his face and chest.

"Well, you're just full of fucking surprises!" Mr. Brackstone screamed up through the trapdoor.

He took a minute to regain his composure. Then, very gingerly, he headed back up the ladder into the room. This time, he held his hands in front of his face for protection, in case she had anything else to throw at him. Colette sat defiantly against the wall in a puddle of her own urine, her hands covered in her own waste.

"Well, it looks like somebody had a little accident," Mr. Brackstone said in disgust while holding his nose.

He picked up the gallon jug of water and cleaned his face off. Then he poured the remaining water onto the floor where Colette had relieved herself. The mixture of urine and water seeped through the small openings between the wooden plank floorboards yet offered no relief from the smell of fresh human waste which permeated the miniscule room. Colette cupped a small amount of water in her hands and cleaned them off quickly.

"Oh, how the mighty have fallen," Mr. Brackstone whispered, watching his hostage licking the remaining clear water off the floor. Mr. Brackstone threw the empty jug at Colette and exclaimed, "You try some stupid trick like that again, Colette, and the next video I make of Tom and Mat is going to be their execution. Do you understand me, young lady?"

Colette stopped foraging the ground for water. She looked up at Mr. Brackstone in shock. She had truly believed Mr. Brackstone was trying to play head games with her earlier.

"Let me see the tape then," Colette demanded in her most hateful voice.

"Surely, Colette. Just let me set it up for you."

Mr. Brackstone pulled out the small LCD screen on the video camera and rewound the tape. He flipped the camera around and hit Play. Colette's eyes grew wide and filled with tears at the sight of Mat and Tom stuck at the bottom of the elevator shaft. She saw Mat saying something on the screen, but Mr. Brackstone had the volume turned off. She could make out the words "I love you" from his lips, however.

In a faint, surrendered voice, Colette lovingly said, "I love you too, Mat."

Mr. Brackstone closed the LCD screen.

"Aw, isn't that cute. I guess you two really do have feelings for each other. I guess that puts you in a dreadful situation. You see, with just the push of a button, that old cargo elevator goes down to the basement. Unless your friends are made out of solid rock, they aren't going to fare too well against that old iron thing. So you should really think about the way you want to treat me. I have those boys in the palm of my hand, I can crush them whenever I choose. So think very carefully about what you say to me, Colette."

Colette struggled to her feet. Her knees wobbled from her severe lack of energy. She dropped her head in defeat and uttered the unthinkable words: "You win, Mr. Brackstone. I will do whatever you want. Anything you ask of me. On one condition: you don't kill my friends."

Mr. Brackstone could not believe his oversize ears. He twirled around in jubilation. Finally, everything he had worked for was coming to fruition. The ultimate goal in his sinister plan had just been placed upon a silver platter at his feet. Mr. Brackstone walked over to his hostage, extending his skinny hand.

"It's a deal then, Colette. I promise I will not kill those boys as long as you do whatever I want. And when I say whatever I want, I really mean that. If you so much as complain once about the things I ask you to do, I will squash those boys like a couple of grapes. No more defiance, no more attitude. You have to take what I give you and like it, young lady."

The once overly proud prom queen unclenched her fists.

"Yes, sir, anything you want."

Colette could not believe what she was about to do. She reached her trembling hand out and shook Mr. Cliff Brackstone's bony hand. An immoral deal with the devil was sealed. Colette's hope of rescue faded away through the evil covenant of a true madman.

CHAPTER 27

Unopened Doors

Two blocks from the clock tower, Branch and Mildred fumbled and searched through countless documents like a couple of mindless cockroaches searching for a steak in a dumpster full of cardboard. Anything that could be considered a clue as to the whereabouts of Mr. Brackstone or his victims would be a major break in the case at this point. They were at a standstill, and Mr. Brackstone was still only a suspect; they had no pure evidence he killed any of the girls from Mildred's list. The dead priest was the only solid thing they had on Mr. Brackstone.

"This is hopeless, Mildred. We have been looking through this chicken scratch for hours, and we've come up with absolutely nothing."

"Well, that's a really positive outlook on the situation. Hell, why don't you just pack up and go home then?" Mildred responded.

"I just might do that, Agent Wiseass. And in the meantime, I'll hand in the biggest screw job ever performed on a case to clear my own ass, how does that sound?"

"I'm sorry, Branch, I'm just a little fried."

Branch tossed the files back into a dusty cardboard box and stormed out to the street in frustration. Mildred followed him out to try to clear her head as well. The two FBI agents sat on the steps of the police station. Looking down Main Street, they could see the local people going about their daily business. A group of South American illegal immigrants nervously walked out of sight.

Branch pulled out a small box of white mints and offered one to Mildred. She took the curiously strong mint, revealing her seldom-seen smile to her partner. The case had reached its greatest decline. They both knew nothing in those files would help them locate Mr. Brackstone at this point. He was a hundred miles away by now, or possibly right under their noses. The clock tower's chiming bells obliterating the thoughts in their wandering minds, both of the agents looked up to the historic stone tower which showed the time being seven o'clock in the evening.

Branch turned to Mildred and mentioned, "If we are going to continue looking over all of this junk, we're going to need some serious caffeine. Want to join me for some coffee? It's on the bureau."

Mildred replied in an agreeable manner, "I don't think coffee is going to do the trick for me. I think I need some boost."

"What the hell is boost, Mildred?"

Mildred smiled again and helped her partner off the stairs.

"Boost, my friend, is the lifeblood of this little town. I guess the best way to describe it would be a really flat pitch-black Coke with ten times the amount of caffeine. It is extremely addictive. If you drink enough of it, you can stay up all night and then some."

Branch made a sour face and replied, "Oh, that sounds really tasty, Mildred. I swear, people on this side of the river think of some really weird shit to do with their free time. But hey, I'll try anything that's going to give me that kind of energy right now."

They walked across the street into the local newspaper shop. Mildred contentedly poured two oversize plastic cups full of the strange black substance as Branch paid for them. Branch looked a bit worried as he inspected the large plastic glass. Nonetheless, he boldly gulped down his first taste of boost. He curled his lips and sucked his cheeks into his face.

Following a loud cough, he looked at Mildred and began, "What did you say was in this stuff? Oh my god, it tastes like syrup and ass!"

They both laughed hysterically then headed outside again and sat on a bench facing the police station. Branch's cell phone vibrated against the wood.

He flipped opened the phone and talked.

"Branch here."

"Hey, Branch, it's Tyler. Listen, I ran a spectral analysis on the DNA from the teacher's room. It's worse than we thought. We now have hard evidence on twenty different DNA patterns. We can try to cross-reference the patterns with any local samples from the list you've given me. But that is going to take a lot of time and money. I'm going to need you to 'okay' the work if you want it done, Branch."

Branch sighed into the phone.

"That's okay, Tyler. I'm sure we are going to have plenty of time to run all of those tests once we have our suspect. I need you to keep searching for more evidence over there. Something out of place, anything that we can use to find this sick asshole. I'm counting on you to give me a lead here, Tyler. We are all out of options over here."

He flipped his cell phone shut. Frustrated and tired, Branch took another sip of boost. The two agents sat side by side quietly. The chances of catching Mr. Brackstone before he killed Colette were growing slimmer by the hour. Both of the agents knew the harsh reality that it would soon be a body-recovery case.

With no more leads and no witnesses, they had nothing to go on. No direction to look. So they sat on the bench, looking up at the clock tower, feverously sipping boost, wondering if they would catch a break and be able to stop Mr. Brackstone's reign of terror. Branch stood up and walked over to the trash can. He threw out the remaining boost.

Turning to Mildred, he issued, "Well, Agent Mildred Beron, I have had absolutely no sleep since this whole thing started. I don't think I am going to be much use to this case until I get some rest. Nothing against your boost, but I'm still tired as hell. So you can walk back to that little shit shack of a hotel we are staying at, or you can go back into that police station with Barney and look through old case files till your eyes fall out of your skull."

Mildred hopped up off the bench and took Branch's arm.

"I think I'll get a couple hours in myself, Agent Branch. Besides, I can't let you walk home alone. You might get lost in this big town."

"Hell, Mildred, I've had women in my life bigger than this town."

"I wouldn't brag about that if I were you, Branch."

The two laughed and headed down the road. Little did they know, perched high above them, Mr. Cliff Brackstone subtly watched their every move down the street. Through his telescope, he inspected the agents' every step as they glided down Main Street and turned the corner. They neared the hotel. Mr. Brackstone gripped his telescope tightly in silent anticipation of what was to come.

Branch got to his door and fumbled with his keys. Mildred followed him up next to the door. She pressed her breasts firmly against Branch's muscular chest.

"The way you're dragging around looking through those keys, someone might think you're drunk, Branch." Mildred flipped back her hair in a flirtatious manner. "Maybe you would feel better over in my room?" Mildred suggested as she took a hold of his muscular arm.

Branch looked into Mildred's eyes. She had the look of a very lonely woman. Everything Branch had been taught at the academy told him to never get involved with another agent while working on a case. He took Mildred's hand and removed it from his arm.

"We have to stay frosty on this, Mildred. People's lives are at stake. You know we can't do that. We let our guard down for one second, and we might let our personal life get in the way of catching this raving psychopath."

Mildred pulled away from him.

"Oh, yeah, I get it." She turned the rusty birth-marked side of her face away from Branch in defiant shame.

"I know I'm not much to look at. I don't know what I was thinking. You probably get girls that look like models throwing themselves at your feet."

Branch put his hand on her chin and forced her face back around to look at him.

"That's not it at all, Mildred. Look at me. You are a wonderful woman. If the situation were different, I would take you up on that offer in a heartbeat."

Mildred looked down to the ground, a little bit embarrassed, then turned back around to face Branch with glassy eyes.

"You're not bullshitting me, are you, Branch?"

"I'll tell you what, girl. After we catch Mr. Brackstone and become Riverside heroes, I'll take you out for a big steak dinner. Then we can go dancing over in Philly and show everyone how the FBI gets down," Branch said, giving a little wiggle to his hips.

Mildred laughed at her tired partner dancing in front of his hotel door. She reached up and gave him a big hug.

"You're a good guy, Branch. Even though you need some help on those moves. I'll tell you what, it's a deal. As long as you promise to let me lead if you're going to dance like that."

Branch gave Mildred a serious look and warned, "Don't talk about my moves, girl. I'll dance anyone's ass right off the floor. Including *you*!"

Branch smiled at her then opened the lock on his cheap plywood hotel room door.

"I'm going to grab a couple hours' sleep, then I'll come wake you up, and we'll go get this bastard."

Mr. Brackstone perched high upon the tower like a scheming gargoyle. He squeezed his telescope and focused in on the agents. Branch slowly pushed his door open. A heat of anticipation raged in Mr. Brackstone's soul, and his eyes widened to take in his plan realized.

A strange snap echoed, and the air whistled as Branch forced the door open. The offbeat sounds were accompanied by a flash of fire-engine red in front of Branch's shocked face. Mr. Brackstone smiled from ear to ear as he watched. An old warehouse ax that had been tied off to a crude but effective pendulum on the ceiling swung down and plunged into Agent Branch's abdomen. Mr. Brackstone rolled in psychotic laughter and glee on the stone rooftop.

The pain was immediate. It felt as though his internal organs had all exploded. Mildred watched in shock as her partner writhed in pain with an old fireman's ax stuck into his bloodstained stomach.

Blood gushed uncontrollably from the open wound. Branch looked at Mildred and attempted to speak, but blood took the place of words and rushed out of his mouth like an open faucet. Mildred called for help immediately and tried to aid her wounded partner. She placed her arm around Branch, trying to make him stand still, then began to draw the ax out of his stomach. Branch quickly stopped her.

"Don't pull it out, Mildred. If you pull it out, all of my insides are going to come with it."

Branch spit up blood all over himself and tried to go on.

"Mildred, he must still be around. He may even be watching. Go to the main office and look for the security tape."

"I can't just leave you here like this, are you nuts?"

"Just do as I say, Agent Beron. This is the break we have been waiting for."

Mildred wiped the blood from his face and screamed for help. Branch Agent Branch started going into convulsions. It took all her strength just to hold him up until help arrived. Once the ambulance and emergency medical technicians showed up, Mildred darted to the main office of the hotel.

Mr. Brackstone had regained his composure and been watching the two agents' mortal struggle. He was ecstatic that his trap had sprung so successfully. He danced on the rooftop of the old clock tower, absorbed in his own evil deeds. He went back over to his telescope and watched as the rescue workers cut the ax handle in two. They carefully put Agent Branch on a movable stretcher with the ax still embedded in his stomach and rushed him off to the local hospital. Mr. Brackstone spoke to himself in a devilish tone while standing on the edge of the clock tower rooftop.

"I am unstoppable. Mind over strength. Intellect over brawn. There is no way to deny it: I am the fittest and the strongest. I will take what I want in life. No one can help those who stand in my way. Evolution has created me, the ultimate predator. Look upon me and fear. Mr. Cliff Brackstone is the name of your doom!"

Mr. Brackstone went back to viewing his malicious masterpiece in reasonable comfort. At the same time, Mildred found an available VCR and popped in the hotel's security tape. It was hard to believe that Mr. Brackstone could sneak in right under everyone's noses and set a trap like this. She rewound the tape for a couple of minutes. Then, she saw someone walking along the front of the hotel. She played the scene back at regular speed. It was a pizza deliveryman. She almost continued to rewind past him, but she noticed it was Branch's room he was knocking on. With the cunning of a cat, the pizza man quickly picked the lock in front of him and entered the room. She fast-forwarded thirty minutes later, and he exited the room with no more pizza box. The pizza man walked toward the camera as he exited the hotel but stopped right before he got out of the picture. He raised his head up and took off his pizza delivery hat. Mr. Brackstone's unsightly, blemished face looked into the video screen as if he knew Mildred was going to be watching this after the fact. He smiled and waved, mouthing the words "*bye-bye!*" And an instant later, he was gone.

CHAPTER 28

Dumb Luck

MILDRED FORWARDED ALL THE EVIDENCE she had scratched up to Tyler and the science team. She was alone again in her hunt for the demon of her past and the monster of her present. Her eyes grew tired as if an unseen force were dragging her eyelids together. She could barely flip the pages of the endless files she searched through. It was close to the midnight hour now. She had been searching through the remaining files at the police station, hoping for a shred of evidence on Mr. Brackstone's possible location. Just as she was about to fall asleep on the stack of papers lying in front of her, an idea came to her.

"If he's still around watching and stalking people, then he must be watching me. I bet that old fireman's ax would have had my name on it if Branch hadn't shown up. I need to find a way to draw him out. A way to make myself the bait."

Mildred walked out of the police station doors and down the steps. She cruised down Main Street, looking for the perfect spot. The large green bench outside the newsstand would do nicely. She propped up a couple of papers along with her coat and sprawled out on the bench. She was so tired that it wasn't going to be a problem trying to fall asleep. She settled her head in and snuggled herself into a comfortable position. Then, as if inviting death to her front door, she closed her eyes.

Mildred could still see Branch's tortured face intertwined in her thoughts. The look of pain and astonishment he had was burned into her soul, surely something she will never forget. He always seemed so cool and confident, but in that instant, he was reduced to a bloody, blubbering victim. She shrugged the flashing nightmare off with a cold shiver and slipped unwittingly into a deep sleep.

*****

Mr. Brackstone could not believe his luck. He had watched Branch fall into his trap. Now Mildred lay motionless on a street-side bench just underneath his stealthy hideout, sleeping like a child and ripe for the picking. He put his telescope down and pondered on whether to take the bait or leave this one alone.

"A challenge of the wits you've placed before me, is it? Mildred, I didn't think you would do something this bold. It seems you *did* grow up to be a strong one. I should have killed you when I had the chance. But no worries, my sweet little rusty princess. I can take care of that little mistake right now."

Mr. Brackstone hurried down the rickety backstairs of the clock tower. The dust of a couple of decades kicked up around him, wrapping him in a shroud of dirt in his delightful descent. He scurried into the aged loading docks situated directly behind the tower. That's where he had stashed the boys' pickup truck. He hopped in and hot-wired the old clunker with little effort. The heavy-duty engine fired loud and powerful. The truck raged out to the street, peeling its wheels out of the dusty driveway. Mr. Brackstone brought the mighty truck to a standstill. He peered down the midnight street to see if Mildred was still slumbering on the bench.

She was only two blocks away and still sleeping out in the open midnight's haze. Mr. Brackstone idled forward, floating down the road like a lurking tiger. He turned the headlights off to conceal his movements. He crept closer. Mr. Brackstone gripped the wheel, turning his white knuckles a thick bloodred. He became enthralled with the self-perceived mind game.

"A game of life and death, Mildred. Get ready to lose. You may be bold, but I am wicked."

He punched the gas pedal firmly to the floor. The truck raced down the street; its large steel bumper aimed directly at Mildred on a path of the arcane. As he grew closer, the old truck grew louder. The old V8 thundered under the hood of the rusted Chevy pickup truck. The monstrous steel beast barreled toward its helpless victim. An unstoppable steel giant with a devil at the wheel, bent on the taste of Mildred's blood. A moment before impact, Mildred heard the rumbling engine and opened her eyes.

She saw the accelerating truck closing in on her but only had time to drop to the ground and flatten out. The truck rammed into the bench and ripped it from its bolts. The lifeless green wood flew across the sidewalk and smashed against a brick wall, sending shards of green splinters into the air like confetti. An extended pipe from the exhaust system dragged across Mildred's chest and ripped her open like a ripe tomato. She watched in awe as the old, jacked-up Chevy rolled over top of her. It crossed over into the next street and spun one hundred and eighty degrees. She checked her wound quickly but felt a puddle of blood where her left breast once resided. Her other hand instinctively pulled out her Glock nine millimeter and aimed it at the truck. She let two shots fly into the back of the pickup. One of the shots shattered the back window into a million pieces. The other bounced off the tailgate and careened into the local bank window, setting off the burglar alarm. Mr. Brackstone spun the old truck around again to avoid the harsh onslaught of bullets. He came to a screeching halt in front of Mildred.

Mr. Brackstone looked madly at his wounded prey lying in the street. He threatened his advance, with one foot on the brake and the other revving the engine. Mildred sat up and took careful aim at the dark shadow hunched over in the driver's seat. Mr. Brackstone released the brake and peeled the rear tires. Mildred opened fire on the pickup, shattering the front windshield with her first shot. The old Chevy closed in on her in a matter of seconds. It plowed into her chest unmercifully, launching her limp body into the air. She met the pavement on the other side of the street harshly, rolling head over heels at least five times before coming to a brutal halt against a well-built brick wall. Mr. Brackstone checked himself for bullet holes frantically.

"You missed, Rusty. Ha ha ha! You fucking missed!"

Mr. Brackstone floored the old Chevy once again. Mildred struggled to her knees and awaited the final blow that would take her life. Just as all hope faded in her spirit, just before Mr. Brackstone delivered the death blow to poor, unfortunate Mildred Beron, Mr. Brackstone's truck blurred into crunching metal, sideswiped by a police cruiser.

Branch's old friend Barney heard the alarm going off and saw what was going on. He rushed to the scene and, through sheer dumb luck, saved Mildred's life. The truck flipped over once and landed on its side. The airbag from the police cruiser smashed the young policeman's head into the side of the cruiser's window, knocking him out cold. Mildred dragged herself over to check on Barney. She pulled the radio off his chest and called for backup then trained her gun on the truck and issued a warning.

"Mr. Cliff Brackstone, come out with your hands up. If you are unable to move, that's good, because you deserve it, you sick fuck."

It took about two minutes for help to arrive. Tyler had been working late on the case and responded first to the distress call. He checked on Mildred first.

"You okay, Mildred? I got more backup and an ambulance on the way, so just stay still, all right?"

"Tyler, we've got him. He is in that truck. Be incredibly careful, if he moves in the slightest wrong way, put a bullet in him."

"All right, Mildred, I'll check it out."

Tyler took Mildred's gun and crept over to the wrecked truck. He nervously walked behind it and looked through the cockpit. Silence filled the night. Mildred looked on, wide-eyed.

"Tyler, what's going on back there?"

"There's nothing here. Nobody is back here, Mildred. It's empty. Not so much as an article of clothing. It looks like we lost him again."

Mildred looked shocked.

"What do you mean it's empty? Look again. Find a blood trail and follow it. Do something before he gets away, Tyler!"

"You know I can't leave an agent down. I have to wait here with you until help arrives. So calm your ass down and don't make any of your injuries worse. Don't worry, Mildred. He won't be going too far after a wreck like that. I found a good amount of blood in that front seat. So that means our boy is wandering around Riverside, bleeding and hurt. I'm sure that sick bastard will turn up laid out somewhere."

*****

Mr. Brackstone hurried down a backstreet, dragging his left leg behind him. A large piece of glass from the passenger-side window dug deeply into his skinny thigh. He held his hand over the wound to try to control the bleeding. With every step he took, the burning hunk of glass sank deeper into his leg. He limped as fast as he could into the loading docks behind the clock tower. Whimpering like a wounded dog, Mr. Brackstone picked up a small wooden board next to him and bit down on it, preparing for the worst. He thrust his fingers into the gaping wound and grabbed the jagged shard of glass. With one swift pull, he dislodged the crimson-colored glass from his quivering leg. He tied off the wound with an old necktie that was folded up in his back pocket.

Mr. Brackstone scurried back to his safe haven, arriving in the security of his clock tower moments later. The police sirens echoed all throughout the sleeping town. Mr. Brackstone got lucky, and he knew it. The wounded maniac huddled down in the basement of the building. He pulled some soggy cardboard boxes around him to shield himself from view. Once he felt snuggly tucked away, he passed out on the floor. Cold thoughts of hatred danced through his plotting mind. With absolutely nothing to lose, a wounded monster took his rest.

CHAPTER 29

Partners Again

MILDRED SLOWLY AWOKE THE NEXT morning to an old gray-haired doctor softly touching her forehead. She tried to sit up but felt an unpleasant pain in her lower back. Wincing in pain, Mildred quickly flopped back down on the hospital bed. Her hand groped at her left breast, hopefully feeling it still intact. It was, though she could feel a long trail of surgical staples running down the center of it. The doctor looked into Mildred's eyes with his penlight and then spoke in a calming voice, "You are a very lucky person. Most people who get run over twice wind up in the bottom of this hospital."

"Where am I? What's wrong with me? Did they catch him?"

"Well, you are at the University of Pennsylvania Hospital. You have a hairline fracture in your tailbone. That fracture is situated on the little bone that sits at the top of your butt. You also have a very acute scar across your left breast. Not to mention a lot of road rash all over your body. I don't know who you were chasing, dear, so I can't answer the last question."

Mildred struggled up to her elbows, wincing in pain all the way.

"Well, I don't feel all that bad. Can you please get me my cell phone so I can make some calls?"

"I can do better than that, young lady. Just wait a minute."

The kind doctor left the room and sent in the armed guard who was stationed outside the door. A portly agent walked over to Mildred's bedside.

"I am Senior Agent Wood. I have been assigned to protect you and Agent Branch from any further attacks."

"Agent Branch. You mean he made it? Is he okay?"

"He is fine, Agent. The doctors say he will make a full recovery. Now, we need to know what happened to you, Agent Beron."

"I was attacked by Mr. Cliff Brackstone. Since you're asking me what happened, I guess they didn't catch him. I need to get up. I have to get back on the case. What is the agency doing now?"

The portly agent placed his hand on Mildred's shoulder, pushing her firmly back to the bed.

"You are off this case, Agent Beron. Effective immediately. This case has been reassigned to me, and we are broadening our search for Brackstone. We figure he hightailed it out of the area after his assault on you and Agent Branch. Any intelligence that you have not communicated to us needs to be sent to the main office as soon as possible. I will accompany you back to Riverside. We will find your research, but in no way, shape, or form are you to pursue this man any further. Do you understand me, Agent Beron, or do I need to take your gun and badge on this one?"

"I understand you, sir. I would like to see Branch before we leave, if that is possible?"

"Sure thing, Agent. Just try not to get him excited. They say he isn't out of the forest yet."

Agent Wood flipped her clothing onto her lap and exited the room. Mildred struggled to her feet. Working through the road rash, bumps, and bruises was easy. But with the unbelievable pain of a broken tailbone, she took at least ten minutes to get dressed. Mildred felt like a failure. She had two clean shots at Mr. Brackstone and didn't end it. Looking at her gun, she questioned her own abilities as an agent.

"Why couldn't you have just shot him in the head? Then this nightmare would all be over," she said to herself.

Mildred holstered her weapon and went out to the fluorescent lights of the hospital hallway. Agent Wood took her down the hall to the intensive care unit. He pointed her toward a dark room that soon was illuminated by several green computer screens hidden behind the dull gray bed curtains. Branch's twisted body lay in the middle of a hospital bed. He looked horribly mangled, surrounded by a spider's web of tubes and electrodes poking into his swollen skin. His abdomen stained red, heavily bandaged and drenched in sweat. A large amount of blood could be seen through the otherwise opal-white bandages directly in the center of his belly. Tears came to Mildred's eyes looking at the once-proud man reduced to this.

"Don't cry for me, Mildred. From what they told me, you're the one who missed that motherfucker."

Branch whispered over the beeping machines which his mangled body was hooked up to. Mildred walked over to her wounded friend. She took his flaccid hand into her own and smiled.

"You don't need to worry about that anymore, Branch. We are officially off this case. Besides, I don't think we are in any condition to chase anyone down right now."

"Off the case. Hell, Mildred, you can still walk, can't you? Don't let them take you off this thing. You get another shot at his ass, and I'll put money on it, he's one dead mother. You have to make this thing right for both of us, Mildred. I'm on the bench, but you can still stop him. You can make a difference."

"What am I supposed to do, Branch? They told me I'll lose my badge if I pursue this thing."

"Girl, do you know how many times they've told me that? Don't listen to all of that bullshit. You make this thing right. I think you're the only one that can. Now tell me, what are they doing to find him now?"

Mildred looked out to the hallway at Agent Wood. The hefty agent lumbered around, picking his nose as if no one could see him.

"He says they are pushing the search away from Riverside. They think he took off after trying to take me out of the game. But they still want me to go back and take everything we dug up on Brackstone to HQ."

"What about the girl?"

"I think they've written her off. Guess they figured Mr. Brackstone took her out before trying to tag us."

"They might be right on that one, but we can still hope."

"Well, anyway, like I said, they want me back in Riverside."

"That's good, Mildred. Make sure you do that. Give that nose-picking fat ass in the hallway plenty of paperwork to go through. Make sure you buy him some fast food or something like that too. You know, to get on his good side. Then he won't care if you do a handstand naked in the middle of town as long as he gets what HQ wants. I'll tell you another thing. Brackstone didn't go anywhere. He feels comfortable in Riverside. Hell, he took out two FBI agents and is still giving everyone the slip. I'm sure he's feeling real good about his accomplishments right now. So you go back there and find him, Mildred, because he's waiting for you. I'd bet on it."

"Thanks, Branch. Look, I just want to say I'm sorry about what happened. If I didn't take your attention away at the hotel, you could have dodged that trap. In truth, if you never showed up on the case, I would have been the one with the ax in the stomach."

Branch grabbed her hand strongly and insisted, "Don't blame yourself for this, Mildred. You start playing that pity-game bullshit, and you're no good to anyone on this assignment. What happened to me is the work of that sick bastard. If you want to make me feel better, go shoot him in the ass and stop hanging around here bothering me. Anyway, I guess I should have taken you up on that offer. You see what a brother gets for turning down some loving?"

Mildred couldn't help but laugh.

"Okay, Branch, I get the picture. I'll go get him, on one condition…"

"And what would that be, Mildred?"

"You get better, all right?"

"It's a deal. But I don't think we are going to go dancing anytime soon, if that's all right with you?"

"Hey, just get better, you wiseass."

Mildred left the room. Her heart felt heavy in her chest. She couldn't help but feel responsible for everything that was going on. If only she had said something all those years ago… Agent Wood's wonderful way of barking orders snapped her out of her self-pitying daydream. He insisted they get on their way to Riverside. She gathered her composure and hobbled out of the hospital with her new boss, knowing there was very little time left for her to finish what she had started, and possibly save Colette's life.

Agent Wood made a stop on the way back to Riverside at the University of Pennsylvania's psychology ward.

"We have to go talk to Dr. Branford. He is our psychiatric liaison on this cluster-fuck. I forwarded most of the case information over to him already. Hopefully, he will have some answers for us."

Mildred struggled to overcome her newfound pain as they entered the red brick halls of the psychology building. They found their way up to the administrative offices and tracked down Dr. Branford with relative ease. The middle-aged psychologist sat in his brown leather chair, looking over several documents. He seemed to fit every doctor-of-psychology stereotype physically—a large bald head, brownish-gray locks above his plump ears, ugly tin glasses hanging loosely over his round nose, making a curious statement about his lack of academic fashion. He was painfully unaware of the presence of the two FBI agents standing before him.

"Excuse me, Dr. Branford? I don't mean to interrupt you. I am Agent Wood with the FBI. This is Agent Beron."

They both entered his office with their FBI badges hanging open.

"We faxed over some information about a possible social predator in the area. I was told by my headquarters liaisons that you are the best profiler in the area. Can you be of some assistance in our information-gathering process?"

The portly psychologist peered over the crumpled documents he was reading. His curiosity suddenly piqued, he seemed immersed at the agent's entrance into his psychological world.

"Yes, Agent Wood, I received the file on Mr. Brackstone. I just finished reading through it a second time. You seem to have a very sick boy on your hands."

"What do you mean by that, Doctor?"

Dr. Branford dropped the file on the desk and took a very serious tone.

"Well, how much do you two know about Freud's concepts on mother-son relationships?"

The agents stood in silence with puzzled looks on their faces as if Dr. Branford had just spoken to them in some long-dead language that no one could understand.

"Absolutely nothing, I see. So, I think I need to do a little explaining. I will put it all in very simple terms and do away with all of our psychological wording for your benefit. Mr. Brackstone was obviously abused as a child by his mother. Her abuse ranged from mental to physical. I would imagine somewhere in the furthest reaches of Mr. Brackstone's mind, he remembers every such occurrence. You see, Mr. Brackstone is stuck in a mental time warp. His only confederate in the world was his dog. And his faithful dog killed his mother, ending the actual real-time abuse a long time ago. However, the mental scarring and memories of what that beast of a woman did to him will not fade in his mind. Are you with me so far?"

Both agents nodded their heads in affirmation.

"Good. Now, the list of victims you sent me is the really interesting part of this. Every one of them is socially unacceptable in the physical sense of existence."

Agent Wood looked puzzled. He inquired further, "What does that mean, Doctor? In laymen's terms, if you don't mind."

"That means they were all either deformed, overweight, or physically unappealing. Social rejects, in other words."

Mildred looked down at the ground in shame, turning her birthmark away from the bluntly spoken doctor.

"Oh. I am sorry, Agent, I didn't mean to offend you. Like I was saying, from the report I read, it seems that Mrs. Brackstone was also physically deformed. So you see, Mr. Cliff Brackstone is not attacking these girls out of pure hated for them, or a need for sexual gratification. He is avenging his childhood. He put himself into a power position with these physically deformed young girls. They take the place of his mother. He probably has had a sexual relationship with all of his victims."

"So you're saying this sick bastard was pretending he was sleeping with his mother?" Agent Wood uttered in ignorance.

Dr. Branford seemed to grow irate but continued in a pompous tone. "No, Agent Wood, that's not it at all. The sexual part is about

144

power. In his mind, he finally has power over his mother in these situations."

Mildred interrupted Dr. Branford quickly.

"So what do you think he did with these girls? What is his goal?"

The doctor pulled out an old black-and-white police photo of Mr. Brackstone's mother lying on the kitchen floor. Her deformed body sprawled out in a pool of blood with flesh ripped to shreds dangling from her neck.

"This is his goal, Agent. To be free of the monster that destroyed his youth. To have power over his mother once and for all. You see, Mr. Brackstone's mind is stuck in a nightmare that does not end. He will never stop killing. I guess you could say he was brought up to do it."

Mildred seemed confused. She pulled out a picture of Colette Jennings and handed it to Dr. Branford.

"That's all good to know, Doctor. But if he is replacing his mother with these deformed girls, then why did he just abduct this beautiful prom queen?"

Dr. Branford scratched his head and thought for a moment. His face dropped as he realized the answer.

"Oh my god… This is amazing! It seems that Mr. Brackstone is finished with his struggle. There may be a subconscious part of him that knows what he is doing is wrong. He is surely at odds with himself now. He knew that this girl would be missed. I think our boy is trying to bring a horrible end to his existence on this earth, and he wants to take something beautiful with him."

Dr. Branford paused for a moment as he looked at the picture of Colette.

"You know, there is a good chance that he is still very close to Riverside. I don't see him running away to finish this. He is way too comfortable at home. I would keep a close eye on the city of Riverside, agents. I bet he is still there."

"Well, Doctor, our headquarters came up with an 80 percent probability that this man has already fled the area," Agent Wood remarked.

The short man scratched his bald head and took a deep, cleansing breath. He crumpled the file papers he had in his hand and pointed to the misplaced agent on the other side of the room, stating, "Agent Wood, you came here for my opinion. Those computers you bank so heavily on do not understand the psychology of a man like Mr. Cliff Brackstone. I have spent my entire professional life working with these cases. So if you want to take the advice of a computer over mine, that is your error, sir."

"I'm sorry, Dr. Branford. I just want to get all the angles on this for my report. I assure you we will take your opinion into careful consideration on this matter, and we thank you for all of your time. Is there anything else you can tell us about Mr. Brackstone?"

Dr. Branford walked over to his television set in the corner of the room. He pulled out a videotape from an old evidence box and placed it into the player.

"I found this in our archives. You see, when a child is subjected to a murder scene, there is always a mental health professional called in to check the victim's mental state. Most of the time, the session is videotaped for hospital records. I figured it was worth a look, so I searched a bit and came up with this. It is a bit grainy, not like the digital stuff we are used to now. Though I think you'll get the picture I'm trying to paint for you."

He hit the yellow Play button on the VCR, and the television flickered on. An old black-and-white picture emerged. It contained an amazing look into the past of a psychotic. Mr. Cliff Brackstone as an eleven-year-old boy emerged as the tape cleared itself. He had a fresh, heaping red wound on his face. The young boy sat perfectly still in an uncomfortable steel chair, sipping on some hot tea. A woman's voice could be heard off camera talking to Mr. Brackstone. She began, "Clifford, I am a friend with the state. I have to ask you some really tough questions now about what happened, all right?"

Mr. Brackstone remained motionless and stared blankly into space.

"Clifford, what happened tonight? Did your mother hit you?"

He nodded his head in confirmation.

"Is this the first time she has hit you?"

Mr. Brackstone shook his head no.

"Why did your dog attack your mother, Clifford?"

Mr. Brackstone dropped his head and shrugged his shoulders.

"Why did your dog continue to attack your mother for so long, Clifford? Why didn't you call him off?"

"My name is Mr. Brackstone."

"Oh, I'm sorry, Mr. Brackstone. Can you tell me what happened?"

Mr. Brackstone remained silent.

"Mr. Brackstone, we need to know this, it is very important that you tell us everything that happened tonight. So, I'm going to ask you again. Why didn't you call your dog off?"

The young boy snapped out of his empty gaze and looked into the camera, portraying the true face of hatred. Mr. Brackstone's cold stare sent chills down the agents' spines. Mildred couldn't believe a boy so young could obtain a stare of such hatred.

With the tiresome tears of a tormented youth, he uttered the chilling, unforgettable response, "Why the fuck would I do that, bitch? She got what she deserved. Now she will never hurt me again. I am free."

The social worker stepped into the shot and walked over to Mr. Brackstone. She tried to put her arms around the boy to comfort him. As soon as she touched the terrified youth, he went wild. He clawed and spit at the woman who was swallowed up in a screaming tornado of frustration.

"Don't touch me! Don't touch me!"

He ripped handfuls of hair from the well-meaning woman's scalp. She fell to the ground as Mr. Brackstone repeatedly scratched and clawed at her face. Some police officers rushed into the room and restrained the tormented boy. He cried a sound of unequaled grief. Then the tape ended.

Dr. Branford turned off the television. He walked back over to his fine oak desk and plopped into his chair. With all the sincerity he could muster, the intellectual doctor pleaded his case one more time.

"You have to catch this man, and quickly. If I am right about this, he is close to the end. The abused child inside of Mr. Cliff

Brackstone wants it to be over. He just wants to take as many innocent things with him as possible. This girl, Colette, I would say she is either dead already or trapped somewhere being tortured. Go back to Riverside, Agents. You don't have much time left."

CHAPTER 30

The Smell of It

MAT WOKE UP TO THE billowing bells of the clock tower chiming eleven times. He felt his way across the bottom of the dark shaft over to his friend Tom. There was an unfamiliar smell lingering in the moist air. Mat sniffed around, trying to figure out what it was that aroused his senses so eagerly in the small shaft. He put his hand on Tom's forehead and felt a strong heat radiating from his friend's clammy skin. Tom must have developed a strong fever overnight, most likely attributed to the steady loss of blood and sleeping in the cold elevator shaft overnight. Mat turned to inspect his friend's hideously broken leg.

He heard a creepy sound. Crawling his way across the wet floor, he found a large sewer rat chewing on his friend's bloodied pant leg. The small carnivorous creature busily sopped up the dried blood with its vermin devil's tongue. Mat picked up the soggy rat and launched it into the darkness. It squeaked in self-defense. A loud thud ensued, followed by the sound of its dead carcass sliding down the concrete wall. Mat turned his attention back to Tom's wound.

As he grew closer to the injury, the smell grew in strength. Mat held his nose. The disheveled jock thought it smelled like the cheese section at the local grocery store. Looking at Tom's wound in the dark, Mat's eyes had adjusted to the dark well enough to realize a strong infection had set in. If he didn't get his friend to a hospital soon, he would surely die.

Tom woke up just as Mat strengthened the splint around his leg. He cried out like a sorely wounded animal, pleading for Mat to stop touching his wound.

"Tom, I have to cut the blood flow to your leg. You have a bad infection down here, and it will spread if we don't do something."

Tom looked at his friend with rolling tears in his eyes.

"Mat, you have to do something. You have to get us out of here. I'm not going to make it through another night in this dungeon. I don't care if you have to leave me. Just try something."

"Okay. I'll try something."

Mat looked around for an idea of what to do. He took what was left of the wooden ladder and propped it against the shaft wall leading up to the second-floor doors. He climbed the ragged, half-burned ladder holding Tom's tire iron in his pant loops. When he got to the very top of the soot-covered ladder, he thrust the tire iron up toward the door. With luck, it wedged into the joint of the iron doors, and a thin line of daylight breached the darkness of the black shaft.

"You got it, Mat. Keep pushing it open!"

"I'm trying, it won't budge. I need to get higher."

As Mat tried desperately to pry his way to freedom, Mr. Brackstone woke up only fifty feet away. He was curled up in his basement room, still covered by his cardboard disguise. He immediately inspected the tender gash on his leg. Lucky for him, all the glass came out in one pull. If anything was left in the wound, he would have woken up in agony. Mr. Brackstone tied off the necktie firmly and removed the boxes he had piled up around him. Just then, he heard faint noises of excited conversation coming from down the hall. Limping slowly toward the basement shaft doors, he could hear Tom cheering Mat on.

"Push harder, Mat, you're almost there!"

Mr. Brackstone's heart skipped a beat and subsequently raced in panic. He clumsily hobbled up the steps toward the second-floor doors. He couldn't catch his breath fast enough to keep up with his quickening pace. As he rounded the corner, he could see the steel doors opening about half a foot, the end of the tire iron clumsily pulling them apart. Mr. Brackstone limped as fast as he could down the long hallway, dragging his lifeless leg behind him in a panicked limp. He saw a grimy set of fingers pawing at the opening. The emergence of Mat's filthy yet determined face appeared through the shadows into the morning light. The doors opened another foot. Mr. Brackstone leaped at the opening. Mr. Brackstone hit the ground ass first and then slid baseball style with his good leg extended.

His foot smashed against Mat's face, landing firmly on the bridge of the nose. The blow made a vicious cracking noise that echoed down the empty hallways and bounced off the elevator shaft walls. Tom looked up and witnessed the blow hurling Mat through the air into the other side of the shaft. His head slammed against the concrete wall much like the rats must have, and then he plummeted through the darkness once again. The fallen hero landed for the second time in two days on top of his wounded friend, forcing the air out of both of them. Mr. Brackstone struggled to his feet. He looked down the shaft, witnessing the two boys floundering at the bottom, writhing in a painful mass of blood, bones, and bedlam.

"Well, that was a very athletic move. I bet you didn't think I could move that fast. Like I told you little dumb asses before, I am smarter than you two. So, you better hope Colette does what she's told, or you two pissants will pay an exceptionally vicious price."

Tom yelled up the shaft at his capturer, "Why are you waiting, you sick fuck? Get it over with! If you're a real man, you would come down here and take us on, man-to-man!"

"Well, Tom, as inviting as that sounds, I think I'll stay up here with Mat's girlfriend. Nothing against you boys, but I just don't like you that way. Oh, and don't worry, I'll make sure you can't try that little maneuver again. Take your last look at the daylight, fellas."

Mr. Brackstone closed the heavy doors and picked up the control panel he hardwired into the side of the elevator's electrical system. He pressed the green button on the panel. The ancient cargo elevator came to life in a dull hum and then started moving down its malicious path toward the basement. The boys frantically looked around for something to pry against the wall. Mat stood up and clawed at the locked doors like a wild animal stuck in a cage. Tom wedged the tire iron on an iron beam running along the bottom of the shaft and braced for impact. Mat's nose was bleeding profusely, and his hands started bleeding as well. The more he clawed at the unmoving doors, the thicker the blood appeared across his fingertips.

The elevator reached the top of the doors and forced Mat to his knees. The two boys screamed as the elevator rolled unmercifully closer to the bottom, every inch spelling out their impending demise. They both lay down and flattened out as much as they could on the bottom of the shaft. The ancient, corroded elevator loomed over their existence. They felt their lives slipping away as it inched closer by the second. Just before the elevator reached the extended arm of the tire iron, it came to a sudden halt. They both let out a sigh of relief, happy they were still alive.

Mr. Brackstone limped back down the stairs to the basement level. He opened a padlock he had attached to the steel doors. It was extra insurance preventing the boys from prying them open during the night. Then he hit a release button on his hardwired panel, and the doors retreated into the corroded walls. There was only a miniature gap between the bottom of the elevator and the empty part of the shaft below it. Mr. Brackstone turned on his flashlight to inspect the dark area. He saw Mat and Tom sprawled out on the bottom of the shaft, quivering like two wet dogs stuck out in a snowstorm.

"You boys comfortable in there?" Mr. Brackstone asked contemptuously while running his fingers through his greasy spaghetti hair.

Mat looked through the crack at the artificial light shining in on them. He scurried toward it as fast as he could and then thrust his bloody hands toward Mr. Brackstone, grabbing him by the ankle. Mr. Brackstone was in complete shock. He pulled at his leg while hitting Mat in the hands with his flashlight. Mat tugged on Mr. Brackstone's skinny ankle with all his might and sent the slight man crashing to the hard concrete floor. Mr. Brackstone posted his other foot against the base of the elevator in the shaft. Mat's hands were extended out of the shaft, struggling to keep a hold of Mr. Brackstone's squirming leg.

Mr. Brackstone reached out urgently and grabbed the control panel. He pushed the green button. The unmerciful elevator started its unpleasant descent once again. Mat pulled his right arm in quickly, but to his ultimate despair. His left arm got stuck in the shrinking crack. Tom jammed the tire iron in the opening as the elevator began to crush Mat's arm. Mat screamed in pain and tugged at his entrapped forearm. Mr. Brackstone managed to fight back to his feet. He brushed himself off and took a long, thankful breath.

"I told you, boys, you can't outsmart me. It's a shame it had to come to this. Now wait right there. I have to go get something."

The boys feverishly worked at freeing Mat's arm. They could hear Mr. Brackstone foraging around upstairs. Mat tugged as hard as he could, to no avail. His arm was firmly stuck. Mr. Brackstone limped back down to the basement and watched the boys struggle for a minute. He took pleasure in their pain. It made him feel like a powerful man. Mr. Brackstone kneeled down to inspect the boys closer.

"So, are you two ready to give up yet?"

The boys stopped struggling for a second and turned their attention to Mr. Brackstone.

Tom looked out of the small opening and asked, "What are you going to do to us, Mr. Brackstone?"

"You really should have told your friend to compose himself, Tom. Now, what I want you to do is remove that tire iron so he can learn his lesson. I'll stop the elevator before it crushes you. But Mat will be short one arm, of course."

Mat screamed out at Mr. Brackstone, "Fuck you! You are a sick bastard and a weak man. If it really came down to just me and you, I would rip your fucking head off in a matter of seconds, and you know it!"

Mr. Brackstone shook his head at the enraged youth.

"Tom, I'm waiting for your answer."

"What if I don't move it?" Tom asked defiantly.

Mr. Brackstone reached into his back pocket and produced a can of lighter fluid accompanied by a pack of matches.

"If you don't do it, then you both burn."

Mr. Brackstone squeezed the rickety tin can. A firm line of the flammable solution splashed the boys in the face, dousing them with the strong-smelling fluid. Mat spit out some of the fuel that went

153

into his mouth. Tom retreated to the back of the shaft, blubbering like a baby. Mr. Brackstone ran his fingers through his black hair again, waiting for Tom's decision.

"Well, what is it going to be, Tom? Do you want to burn? Or, watch your friend lose a limb? The clock is ticking."

Mr. Brackstone flipped back the matchbook and tore off one of the matches. He placed it against the lighting strip and smiled at Mat's bloody face. Mat turned to his friend and urged him.

"Do it, Tom. I don't want to burn. You know darn well he will do it. He will light that match, and then both of us will go up. So just fucking do it, all right?"

"That's right, Tom, listen to your friend. I will set both of you ablaze. Now get over here and do as your brave friend tells you."

Tom pulled himself back toward the opening. He could hardly catch his breath. His broken leg dragged behind him, striking him with pain every time he made a motion across the shaft. He looked up at Mat and shook his head as if to say he couldn't do it. Mat gave him a stern look, then closed his eyes tight, and shook his head, showing he was ready. Tom grabbed the end of the tire iron and pulled.

As the tire iron tugged loose into Mat's hand, an earsplitting scream penetrated the walls of the clock tower. Mr. Brackstone watched in glorious splendor. The elevator crushed Mat's left arm, tore it off right above the elbow. Mat tugged bravely backed into the shaft until his arm was fully amputated. The elevator then stopped. Mat fell back into the shaft, bleeding uncontrollably from his bloody left nub. Tom took off his shirt and tied off his friend's arm as tightly as he could. The screams of pain were immeasurable on any scale of torture. The bleeding would not stop. Mat soon passed out from the anguish.

Mr. Brackstone picked up the grotesque, amputated arm and inspected it. It was still twitching as if it were fighting to be alive. The bloody fingers seemed to grab after Mr. Brackstone's face in an undying thrust of hatred. He threw the mangled arm into the elevator; it flipped and flopped for a couple of minutes like a fresh fish fighting for life on the shoreline. It finally bled out and came to a somber halt.

Mr. Brackstone closed the doors again. After padlocking the steel doors, he limped back up the stairs, headed toward Colette Jennings with all the worst intentions in mind.

CHAPTER 31

The Key to It All

THE CLOUDS GREW GRAY AS the afternoon dragged on. Agent Wood and Mildred had been going through the old Riverside case files again for about an hour. It was obvious to Agent Wood that Mildred was still in a lot of pain. She toiled through the tedious work begrudgingly as her new boss, and subsequent babysitter, sat close by, being of no help whatsoever.

"You found anything yet, Agent Beron?" Wood asked with a fresh doughnut stuffed in his portly face.

"Not yet, sir, I told you me and Branch already went through this stuff. There is nothing in these files that will help us catch Mr. Brackstone. What we need to do is—"

Wood interrupted rudely before Mildred finished her suggestion.

"What we need to do is keep going through this stuff. HQ put me in charge of this, Agent Beron. If you don't like that, I don't care. This guy has already taken down two agents. I don't plan on being the third. So keep doing the work you are assigned and stop your bitching."

Mildred dropped her head in submission and continued her boring paper search. Wood went back to eating his six pack of doughnuts, adding to his plump figure. A call came over Mildred's phone seconds later.

"Agent Beron, how can I help you?"

"Mildred, it's Branch."

Mildred looked surprised but delighted to hear from her wounded partner.

"You should be resting, not making phone calls."

"Never mind that now. Listen, I remembered something. Back at Riverside High, there was a box of Mr. Brackstone's files in the bottom of his desk. I didn't get a chance to look through them, and I told Tyler's team to leave them for me. I think they are still over there, and I know you are being hamstrung by that fat ass, but you might find something new in them."

"Yeah, good idea, Branch. I will go check it out. Now get off the phone and go eat some Jell-O or something."

"Well, you're welcome, Mildred. Just get on top of that stuff, pronto!"

Mildred hung up and started packing her things to head out. She talked Agent Wood into coming with her, though his sluggish body was reluctant to leave its comfortable chair. They headed down the road to the high school in silence. It was clear that Wood had no respect for Mildred. He kept his eyes trained on the road in front of them so he wouldn't have to make conversation. Mildred didn't mind the silence. It gave her time to think about everything that had transpired so far. She felt lucky to be alive and found a renewed sense of meaning in her search for Mr. Cliff Brackstone. As they pulled up to the school, Agent Wood turned to Mildred and issued some orders.

"All right, Agent, this is how it's going to happen. We are going to go in there, get the files, and take off. These small-town folks have been put through enough. We don't need all these kids talking to their parents about FBI agents hanging around the school all day. Is that clear?"

Mildred looked at her new partner with repugnance and answered, "Yes, sir. Is there anything else, sir?"

"Yes, there is. Don't be a wiseass, Agent Beron."

The odd couple headed into the school. They visited the main office first and informed the principal of their presence. Then they swiftly headed down the hallway to Mr. Brackstone's classroom. As they rounded the corner, the period bell rang out loudly. Students poured out into the hallway, bumping into one another and the agents. The students made childish remarks at the agents as they made their way through the crowd. Mildred had a distinct feeling of belittlement. She felt like she had just time warped back to her oppressive teenage years.

A large group of kids stood huddled around the entrance to Mr. Brackstone's classroom, cheerfully awaiting the agents' arrival. Agent Wood forced his way past the nosy students and cut the police tape strung over the door. He struggled with the lock to the room, while Mildred stood guard over her new partner. From the crowd, Mildred heard a cruel, senseless remark.

"Hey, nice face, freak!"

The huddled students laughed hysterically at the obscene comment. Mildred's eyes filled with rage. She had been gone for so long that she had nearly forgotten the cruelty of teenagers. All the comments and slurs she dealt with as a child in these hallways flooded back to her in an instant. The harsh words rolled around in her mind, badgering her ego, intentionally reminding her of the outcast situation that her own peers placed her in back then— the same situation that gave Mr. Brackstone the power to control his victims. She searched the crowd for the teen who made the comment. The mob parted through Mildred's blank stare as she locked on to him. The handsome young jokester giggled outrageously, slapping his friends and egging the crowd on. With one prompt motion, she grabbed the student by his shirt and slammed him abruptly against the lockers. Mildred put her nose just inches from the young student's face and then screamed, "What do you think gives you the right to talk to people like that! You want me to hall your scrawny ass into jail for obscene comments to a federal officer, son?"

The boy stood submissively, silent and frightened. The sound of dripping water against the hard tile floors of the hallway broke the silence. The young handsome student pissed his pants, and the warm, stench-ridden urine dripped on the tile floor beneath them.

He shook nervously and motioned his head from side to side, indicating his reluctance at any further confrontation with Mildred.

"That's good, pissy pants, because if you make another comment like that, I'll make sure they find a nice, warm bed next to some real hard-ass kids for you down at juvy. Now move along to your next class, you little punk."

The crowd of students quickly disbursed, pointing and laughing at the deposed joker. A short, fat girl looked at Mildred and smiled. She gave her chubby thumbs-up in support of taking down the school jerk. Mildred returned the gesture as the two shared a moment of togetherness only the outcasts know about. Mildred watched the plump girl skip down the hallway, alone in her moment of happiness, followed by her disappearing into a classroom.

"If you're done roughing up the locals, Agent Beron, I would like to get this box of evidence and get out of here."

Mildred gathered her composure. She had forgotten that Agent Wood was even standing beside her.

"Yes, sir. I'm sorry, sir, it's just—"

"Don't worry about it, Agent. I heard what that little shithead said. I didn't see anything. And you didn't do anything. Got it?"

Mildred looked surprised that Wood had a heart.

"Yeah, I got it, sir. Thanks."

They entered the quiet room and retrieved the box from Mr. Brackstone's combed-over desk. They decided to stay put and go through its contents, in case it turned out to be nothing but school papers, which they would have to return later. The scrounging agents were in luck. The box was full of personal documents from Mr. Brackstone's private life. It gave the agents a plethora of vacation receipts, personal pictures, award documents, and other such priceless material to go through. Agent Wood got on his cell phone immediately and relayed information back to HQ as quickly as he could read it.

Mildred seemed uninterested in the obvious clues. There were only a couple of things that stood out to her. There were several flyers stuffed at the bottom of the box asking for donations to save the clock tower in the center of Main Street. A certificate of achievement was mounted on a plaque from the city of Riverside. It read:

The City of Riverside
Awards the Key to the Clock Tower
To: Mr. Clifford Brackstone
For your relentless efforts in restoring, reviving, and bringing new light back to our city's great historical landmark.

Riverside is in your debt.

Sincerely,
Mayor John Henry Miles

Underneath the writing, there seemed to be an empty space where a key once occupied. Mildred thought back to Mr. Brackstone's attack on her in front of the newsstand. She was on the bench for about fifteen minutes before Mr. Brackstone got to her. The clock tower was right across the street. Her eyes grew wide. She had just figured out the mystery of Mr. Brackstone's hiding place. Mildred checked her gun, ensuring it was loaded, and darted for the door.

CHAPTER 32

The Worst Kind of Pain

COLETTE SLUGGISHLY LEANED HER DEHYDRATED body against the rigid wall. Completely famished, for the first time in her life, her entire spirit was sapped of energy, unable to fight. Her soiled and dirty clothes felt damp against her skin. She couldn't even muster the energy to push her tangled hair away from her exhausted eyes. Entrenched in a nervous bedlam, her mind wondered how Mat and Tom were doing and if they were even alive. The thought of giving herself to Mr. Brackstone made her stomach feel ill. Licking her dry lips in a futile attempt at wetting them, Colette realized the blinding truth: Mr. Brackstone was right.

All her power to struggle had vanished. She had become the proverbial sitting duck. There would be no fighting back this time. She had no will for it. Colette made a deal with Mr. Brackstone even though she knew he was going to take her anyway. The reality of what Mr. Brackstone was going to do to her eerily stung her thoughts. She realized there was no way of getting out of this situation alive. If she was going to be rescued, it would have already happened. Subsequently, the once-proud Colette Jennings dropped her head to the hard wooden plank floor and gave up in despair.

Her eyes barely split open, leaving her with blurred vision as she rested her head on the floor. Colette unexpectedly noticed small shimmering shards of shattered glass from the broken picture frame. The multitude of miniscule shards glistened across the floor within her frantic reach. She instantly gathered up the microscopic shards of glass into her trembling palm. And after some effort, her quivering hands produced a small pile of razor-sharp material. She looked at her handful of sparkling shards and thought profoundly. Then, an unthinkably atrocious path sprang into her dark thoughts. A desperate grin emerged across her chapped lips. Colette Jennings realized the unimaginable course she must embark on.

Minutes later, the trapdoor slammed opened. Mr. Brackstone emerged, bloody and limping. He managed his way over to the cot opposite of Colette and flopped down. His wound had stopped bleeding, but Colette could see the bloody tie wrapped tightly around his leg. He ignored Colette for the most part while he inspected the gash on his leg. Reaching into his bag, Mr. Brackstone pulled out a large bottle of painkillers and downed some quickly to take the edge off.

He drank an entire bottle of water in about two minutes, with Colette's dehydrated eyes looking on hungrily. There was a half inch of water remaining in the clear plastic bottle as he tossed it at Colette. She drank the clear liquid quickly and licked at the inside of the cap to ensure she had gotten all the moisture she could. Mr. Brackstone flipped himself around on the cot and waved at Colette.

"Did you miss me, Ms. Jennings?"

Colette hid her head in her chest and remained silent.

"Oh, what's the matter, honey? All the wild fighting drained out of you already? I didn't expect you to break this fast. But, it's a good thing you did. Those boys are going to need some medical attention soon. So you better come through with your promise. Remember, you said you'll do whatever I want."

She looked up at her abductor through her long black hair.

"I will keep my word, Mr. Brackstone. Just remember, you promised not to kill them."

"Yes, I remember, Colette. Don't worry, they are still alive. In fact, I just checked on them. I think your boyfriend even wanted to give me a hand, but I had to decline. This is a one-man job. They seem to still have a great deal of fight left in them though. More than you, that's for sure."

Colette parted her hair slowly and then looked at her abductor with sad yet seductive eyes.

"I have no energy to fight you, Mr. Brackstone. You win. You were right. I have nothing left to wrestle you with."

Mr. Brackstone eerily grinned from ear to ear. His gangly, mis-arranged yellow teeth dripped with saliva in anticipation of his ulti-mate prize. Mr. Brackstone began to disrobe in front of Colette. He slowly removed his shirt, revealing his colorless, acne-infested torso. A few particular zits had risen to extreme whiteheads looking ready to burst at the slightest pressure. He was so skinny; Colette could see every cut of muscle and bone on his grotesquely emaciated rib cage. A large black-and-blue bruise stood out on his chest and another on his ribs. He clumsily pulled off his shoes and then his socks, filling the room with the awful smell of wet feet. Colette backed against the wall in complete fear of what was to follow.

She had never seen a naked man in the flesh, and this was a hell of a way to start. Mr. Brackstone unbuttoned his trousers. They dropped to the floor, exposing his sticklike, pasty, white legs. Colette noticed the gaping wound on his leg and then covered her eyes.

"No, no, no, Colette, you have to watch me get ready. Remember, it's whatever I want."

She parted her fingers slightly, barely exposing her eyes to the horrendous sight in front of her. Mr. Brackstone put his thumbs into his off-white briefs and pulled them down, slowly revealing the dis-gusting brown stains on the backside of them. Colette shivered at the sight of Mr. Brackstone's unsightly naked body. His curved penis and lopsided balls dangled between his legs inauspiciously sheltered in dark black pubic hair. Colette hid her face once again.

"What's the matter, Ms. Jennings? You don't like what you see?" Mr. Brackstone said while laughing. "Now I am ready. It is your turn now, Colette."

Mr. Brackstone walked over to Colette and untied her then sat back down on his cot, fully exposed.

"Get undressed, now!" he ordered in a raised voice.

Colette struggled to her feet, barely able to stand. She brushed her long black hair away from her face, revealing her dirty yet strikingly beautiful features. Little by little, she unbuttoned her shirt then threw her soiled blouse into the corner of the room. She shyly removed her bra, exposing two large milky-white breasts. Even without her bra, they stood firm and perky on the young prom queen's chest. Mr. Brackstone began to feel intensely aroused. He stroked himself evenly while watching Colette disrobe in front of him.

"This is better than I ever imagined. Keep going."

Colette unbuttoned her shorts and peeled them off, exposing her white lacy thong panties. Mr. Brackstone gawked at the nearly naked beauty at his mercy.

"Keep going, Colette," he demanded.

Colette was visibly embarrassed but continued. She slipped off her thong slowly, revealing her most private area to Mr. Brackstone's open perversions. She then swiftly covered her secretive parts with her hands. She stood shivering in front of Mr. Brackstone, stark naked. Her body was toned, shaped perfectly. Every curve of her young frame subtly tempted Mr. Brackstone into a raging hormone. He stood up to frantically inspect his trophy. He walked around her a couple of times to take in the breathtaking sight. Colette shivered at the contemplation of what was to come.

She could hardly stand from exhaustion. Mr. Brackstone carefully walked her over to the cot and laid her down. He caressed her breasts and buttocks over and over, enjoying every second of his sick fantasy. Colette closed her eyes and let Mr. Brackstone touch her in places she barely touched herself. Then, with one quick movement, Mr. Brackstone spread her tense legs, revealing her untouched innocence to his demonic-eyed delight. He kneeled in between her legs, disgustingly stroking his cock.

"You will never forget this lesson, Colette. I will show you what a real man is all about."

Mr. Brackstone spit on his hand and lubed his peculiar penis in preparation. Colette bit down on her bottom lip, preparing herself to be taken. She said a small prayer to herself as Mr. Brackstone thrust his hard penis into her untouched vessel. A howling scream pierced the air and slammed down the long, empty halls of the clock tower. Both of the conjoined agonizers bellowed in a melody of excruciating agony. Mr. Brackstone pulled himself out cautiously, but quickly, revealing the small shards of crimson glass imbedded into his bloody penis. Millions of miniscule holes opened up on his penis as bright-red blood poured into his hands.

He fell to the ground in shock, trying to cut the flow of blood by clamping down on the top of his manhood. Mr. Brackstone's mutilated penis gushed bright-red buckets all over his hands to his ultimate dismay. Colette curled up in a fetal position, holding herself and bleeding profusely.

"You stupid fucking bitch, what did you do!" Mr. Brackstone screamed.

Colette turned to look at Mr. Brackstone reeling on the floor. "I gave you what you deserved, Mr. Brackstone. Did you learn your lesson?"

Mr. Brackstone stood up, enraged. The skinny demon picked up one of his shoes and began beating Colette about the face and neck with it. Colette lay helpless on the cot. With no energy left to fight, she balled up into an instinctual fetal position and allowed Mr. Brackstone to strike her repeatedly. Blood was still gushing from his penis. He whaled on Colette, beating her without mercy. The tortured prom queen seemed to pass out in the middle of the beating. Mr. Brackstone suddenly began to feel a bit light-headed. He stopped his onslaught and managed to get back into his clothes rather quickly. Then, the wounded monster disappeared down the trapdoor. Colette lay motionless on the cot, her face bloody and bruised. Death seemed close to her, her inner conscious wondering if she would ever wake up again.

CHAPTER 33

Repercussions

Mr. Brackstone floundered to the ground at the base of the attic ladder, convulsing in humiliating anguish numerous times. He held his wounded cock tightly as he struggled down the hallway. Approaching the large second-floor elevator doors, Mr. Brackstone grabbed his hardwired remote in hurried anticipation. He maliciously mashed down the green button. The large iron death box started its terrible descent toward the helpless victims lying at the bottom of the solemn torture pit.

The boys heard the looming monstrosity come to life. They began screaming at the harsh realization that the elevator's tarnished brakes had just released above them. The steel bottom inched closer to them by the second, like a bad scene from an old Egyptian *Tomb Raider* movie had come to life before their weary eyes. Its descent was quick, and the boys were soon flattened out on the hard floor once again. The tire iron pressed against the cold metal bottom of the elevator at one end and a long metal beam running across the bottom of the shaft at the other. The sturdy tire tool began to buckle from the tremendous pressure. The boys nervously looked at each other and prayed.

The thin piece of metal bent and began to slip, but Tom firmly held it in place. Both boys held on to the tire iron for dear life. It was the only thing holding back their impending doom. Mr. Brackstone listened for death screams and crushing bone from the second floor but, to his lonely dismay, heard neither.

The wounded maniac hurried down the empty steps toward the basement entrance. A sharp pain snapped at his inflamed penis with every hurried step on his descent. Mr. Brackstone backed against the wall, still standing on the steps, placing his probing hand into his pants; it soon emerged with a shining puddle of glass-chunked blood resting in the palm of his quivering hand. The enraged predator screamed a hatred cry that pierced the frightened ears of his neighboring hostages. He wiped the remnants on his shirt and hurriedly limped up to the elevator, still bleeding horrifically from his inflamed crotch. He unlocked the sturdy padlock which held the large steel doors shut and saw the boys huddled around the tire iron, holding on to it as tightly as they could.

"Ha ha, hello, boys! I have some bad news for you today. It seems Colette went back on her little promise, so unfortunately, you two miscreants are going to pay the callous price. It won't be too cruel. I will even be sporting about it and give you a choice. You can kick that flimsy piece of steel out from under the elevator and make it quick, or I can light a couple of matches and watch you burn to a cinder, nice and slow."

Tom looked out of the narrow slit at Mr. Brackstone and pleaded, "Please, Mr. Brackstone, don't do this! We will do whatever you want. Come on, we never gave you a hard time, we never did anything to you. Don't do this, I'm begging you!"

"Oh, boo-hoo. I don't want to hear you beg for your worthless fucking lives. I want you to choose. Quick and painless, or slow and painful. Which will it be, boys?"

"If you do this, you're going to hell, Mr. Brackstone. There is no redemption for something like this. Think about it, you really don't want to kill us. You have proven your point. We understand now. Brains over brawn. You are stronger than we are. We have learned our lesson."

Mat whispered cautiously, in a blind hope that Mr. Brackstone had some humanity left in his evil soul.

"You haven't learned your lesson yet Mat, that is glaringly obvious. Otherwise, you would have already realized that I don't give a damn about redemption or going to hell. You have learned a little though. So, I am going to give you one last chance at life, boys. Let's see if you were paying attention last week in class. The first question on the test from the last chapter was simple. So if you get it correct, you get to live. If you get it wrong, I'll still let you choose. So without further ado, here is the question: what was the name of the founding father of gravity?"

Tom looked at Mat blankly and shrugged his shoulders. Mat yelled out assuredly, "Isaac Newton! It was Isaac Newton, I remember!"

Mr. Brackstone shook his head and laughed.

"If you two dimwits had paid attention in science class, you would have realized the correct answer is '*Sir* Isaac Newton.' I'm sorry, that is an incorrect answer, boys. Now, choose your demise."

The traumatized teenagers remained completely silent. Mr. Brackstone shrugged and smiled. He then stood up and reached into his pocket, producing a paperback igniter. The raving psychopath tore off a piece of his tattered shirt. Lighting the flimsy piece of cloth on fire, Mr. Brackstone tossed it into the bottom of the dingy elevator shaft. Lighter fluid still drenched the bottom of the damp concrete. It ignited into mindless flames instantaneously. The heartless blaze spread like wildfire over the boys' grief-stricken bodies. They screamed in agony, rolling around on the bottom of the shaft, attempting to smother the flames in a futile dance of death with the raging inferno. The fire boiled their smooth flesh into a bubbling kaleidoscope of blood and flame over a bone canvas.

Mr. Brackstone could see Tom's face begin to drip skin off his very bone. The unfortunate youths pleaded for death while enduring the intense heat of the callous combustion. Mat rolled one more time in an attempt to put out the flames. He dislodged the tire iron in his state of panic. Once released, the heavy creature moved toward its original path of repugnance. It crushed the flames that engulfed the boys' flailing bodies, splattering them into half-inch piles of smoking goo. A horrible stench of smoke and burned flesh rose into the air, engulfing Mr. Brackstone in a truly horrifying haze of inhumanity.

Mr. Brackstone looked on in amazement at the ghastly scene he had just orchestrated. He forgot about the pain between his legs for a second then pressed the control pad once again and sent the corroded elevator back to the second floor. Stepping over to the open doors, Mr. Brackstone looked in with the curiosity of an exploring pioneer. As the smoke cleared, a large smoldering chunk of lifeless flesh and bone peeled off the bottom of the elevator and barely missed landing on Mr. Brackstone's greasy head. A clearer view emerged to his devil eyes. The flames were so hot, combined with the crushing force of the elevator, the two would-be heroes' bodies lay on the bottom, deviously intertwined in a heap of smoking muck. One of Mat's lone eyeballs resting on top of the warm mass was the only human thing recognizable. It stalled Mr. Brackstone for a moment, as though it were staring at him, until it popped from the heated pressure, squirting warm eyeball jelly onto Mr. Brackstone's face. He wiped it off in the midst of insane laughter. The sight and hideous smell of blistering flesh and crushed body parts became too much for even Mr. Cliff Brackstone to partake in. So he turned away from his despicable deed and limped back up the stairs.

Mr. Brackstone made his way in moderation back to the bottom of the trapdoor. His crotch itched and burned so badly he could hardly stand up straight. Looking up through the door, he noticed that his ultimate prize, Colette Jennings, had vanished. His black heart skipped a thundering beat. He peered down the long hallway and picked up a blood trail leading down the empty corridor. He wasted no time in following it. Each step brought more stark pain, which only fueled Mr. Brackstone's hatred for his fleeing victim more. He limped psychotically down the hallway, screaming like a madman.

"Come out here, Ms. Jennings. I didn't give you a hall pass. You're not allowed to just leave whenever you want. I am the boss of this humble establishment!"

He picked up the pace to a slow, awkward run, eager to track down his prey and end her young life. The blood trail led to the back stairwell door. Mr. Brackstone opened the door and rushed down the stairs. He could hear Colette's whimpering voice and heavy steps struggling down the staircase.

"Ms. Jennings, I did not dismiss you, young lady! Now get back up here and *die* like a good girl!"

Colette screamed in fear at the sick, piercing comment. She reached the bottom of the staircase and pushed against the fire exit door. It didn't budge. She slammed her shoulder against it several more times, to no avail. She could hear Mr. Brackstone's crazy ramblings growing closer by the second. She gave the door one final front kick with every ounce of energy she had left. It flew open, revealing the vivid sunlight. The daylight blinded Colette for a second. She ran screaming from the clock tower fire exit, hoping someone would be close enough to hear her desperate pleas.

Mr. Brackstone followed speedily behind her, brandishing an old fire ax from the firebox by the emergency exit. Colette ran as fast as she could. Her tattered clothes hung from her soiled body, barely covering her private areas. An insanely profuse amount of blood trickled down her legs from the self-inflicted booby trap she sprang on Mr. Brackstone. Colette made it up to the train tracks that spiraled in front of the clock tower, but Mr. Brackstone finally caught up to her.

Mr. Brackstone slammed Colette in the back of the head with the butt of the axe. She tumbled to the ground, arousing a cloud of dirt and dust. The helpless victim turned to look at Mr. Brackstone's wild gaze. He lifted the heavy red ax over his head, preparing to strike with all his anger. The rage that encompassed his eyes forced Colette to freeze in fear. She put her hand up to guard herself against the final blow. Mr. Brackstone swung the heavy wooden ax a second too late.

A loud gunshot rang out into the streets. The ax flew out of Mr. Brackstone's hands, jerking him back two feet. He looked across the street in disbelief. Standing on the other side of the road, Deputy George Watson, a.k.a. Barney, stood holding a smoking police-issued shotgun, with a large white bandage over one eye, dressed in his finest Riverside blues.

CHAPTER 34

Delaware Crossing

MILDRED PRESSED HER FOOT TO the gas pedal of the rental car and flew down Main Street, with Agent Wood annoyingly yelling at her to slow down. They rounded the corner to the clock tower and then heard the loud blast from Barney's shotgun. Agent Wood quickly called in for backup. Mildred screeched to a halt on the crossroads twenty yards south of where Mr. Brackstone was standing over Colette. She jumped out of her car and pulled her gun from her holster, aiming it directly at Mr. Brackstone's head. From across the street, she heard Barney yelling for Mr. Brackstone to back away from Colette and lie down on the ground.

Mr. Brackstone looked at the shotgun fixed on him, and then he looked over to Mildred. Their eyes met for the first time in years. Mildred's fears and frustrations came flooding back to her. Some subconscious sliver of her mind was not ready to see him. Her hands began to shake while holding her weapon. The nightmare from her teenage years stood twenty yards away, defiantly staring her in the face. Mr. Brackstone looked at Mildred's shaking hands and then back into her eyes. He smirked and winked at her, sending a frosty chill down her trembling spine. He backed away from Colette slowly, holding his hands up in the air.

Barney ordered him to lie on the ground once again. Mr. Brackstone turned on his heels quickly and made a lightning dash for the fire exit door. A hailstorm of buckshot flew over his head, followed by a loud blast. He luckily stumbled into the stairwell, unscathed.

A sheriff's deputy rushed to Colette's side and embraced her, giving her the first feeling of comfort in what seemed to be ages. Colette was in excruciating pain, but the feeling of safety overshadowed any pain for the moment.

Barney let another shot rain hot lead into the door then gave chase. Mildred flowed into motion. Just steps behind Barney, she ran up to the closed back door of the clock tower where Barney was pressed up against one side of the wall.

"Good to see you're feeling better, Agent Beron."

"Thanks. Listen, I think he has this place pretty well staked out, so expect just about anything in there."

Agent Wood rounded the corner at a lumbering pace, trying urgently to catch his breath while barking orders.

"Agent Beron, backup is on the way. I want you to set up a perimeter around the clock tower."

"But that will give him time, too much time!"

"Do not question my orders, Agent. Set up a perimeter like I said. Coordinate with local law enforcement. I am going to go in and flush him out. I want you to stay in constant radio contact with me. Do you understand your orders, Agent?"

"Yes, sir, but for the record, I think this is a very bad idea."

"Your objection is noted. Now do as I ordered."

Barney took off to the back exit of the clock tower, and Mildred backed away so she could cover the front door and fire exits at the same time. Agent Wood entered the building, sweeping the corners with his gun.

"Agent Beron, this is Wood, come in."

"Go ahead, Wood."

"I have a clean blood trail going up the stairs. I am going to follow it up. As soon as backup arrives, I want you to get up here."

"Yes, sir."

Mildred heard the sirens echoing closer to her position. She couldn't believe she had come this close only to be outranked by some overweight desk jockey who couldn't run twenty yards without panting like a dog. She scanned the doors and windows of the building through her crosshairs, hoping to get a shot at Mr. Brackstone before he was caught. Then, she saw movement between the large brick columns on the roof. She clicked her radio and warned.

"Agent Wood, he went up to the roof. Be very careful, he could have weapons up there."

"I read you, Agent Beron. I want you to call a bird in on this one."

"Roger that, sir."

Mildred radioed in for a chopper. Then she heard a booming gunshot from the rooftop. She started to run toward the stairs but stopped when she saw Agent Wood's plump body emerge between one of the archer's pillars on the roof.

"Agent Wood, are you in need of assistance?"

Only static feedback returned on her radio.

"Agent Wood, come in, are you in need of assistance?"

"I believe Agent Wood is beyond any assistance at this point in his career, Mildred Beron."

Mildred knew the snakelike voice that answered her. Her face froze in horror. It was Mr. Brackstone. She looked up to the stone pillared rooftop. The portly form between the pillars seemed to waddle forward. Agent Wood fell over facedown on the stone opening, revealing a triumphant Mr. Cliff Brackstone standing behind him. Mr. Brackstone bent down and grabbed his legs, flipping him over the boulder-encrusted rooftop. Agent Wood's stout body tumbled down the face of the building, bouncing off the medieval stone crowning in his horrid descent. He smashed against the concrete sidewalk, making a gruesome sound of crushing bone and splattering flesh.

Mildred rushed over to see if she could help her fallen comrade, only to witness a nightmarish, mangled mess. Agent Wood's face crumpled up against the bloody, wet concrete, his body bent over backward with his pelvis thrust up toward the sky. A large piece of his spine stuck up through the bottom of his beer belly, giving ample room for his intestines to sneak out the sides of the gaping wound. She looked up quickly and saw Mr. Brackstone's face hanging over the wall. She took a quick shot with her nine millimeter. Mr. Brackstone's head disappeared quickly.

"Agent Wood is down. I repeat, Agent Wood is down. All law enforcement personnel converge on the clock tower! Take extreme caution when approaching and be aware that Mr. Cliff Brackstone is now armed and considered extremely dangerous. Fire at will if you encounter him."

Mildred stuffed the radio in her belt and ran into the front door of the clock tower. She flew up the stairs, determined to be the one to stop Mr. Brackstone's reign of terror. She reached the roof in record time and scanned every corner and brick with her gun. Her heart pounded through her chest. She could see the fresh puddle of blood on the concrete rooftop. Whether it was Agent Wood's or Mr. Brackstone's, she did not know. Then she heard another booming gunshot from down the back staircase. She ran over to the door and descended the stairs as fast as she could. At the bottom of the stairwell, she saw Deputy George Watson sprawled out on his face. She shrilly flipped his heavy body over. He gasped for air and pulled at the Kevlar vest that had just saved his life.

"Thank God you were smart enough to wear your vest, Barney!"

"I told you, my name is George."

"Sorry, George. Did you see which way he went?"

"Yeah, he went out the door and headed towards the river. Go get that crazy asshole, Mildred."

"You got it, George."

Mildred peeked out the door. She saw fresh blood tracks on the grass leading in the direction of the river. In true reckless style, Mildred gave open chase, knowing full well that Mr. Brackstone had a gun and could be hiding behind any one of the thousands of corners on the way down to the river.

The entire police force of Riverside stormed the clock tower behind her. Mildred heard multiple radio calls for her location. She turned the radio off to secure her position. One by one, she passed the old doorways and dark corners of the back warehouses, wondering if Mr. Brackstone was going to hop out and take an easy shot at her head. She made it through the back posts of the clock tower property. The blood trail continued down a dirt road which led up to the Delanco/Riverside Bridge.

Mildred tracked through the soft sand, wincing in pain from her broken tailbone and severe road rash with every forced step. She stopped for a second and radioed her position in, then quickly turned the device off again. She could hear the helicopter closing in from a distance. The only thing she had to do was get it fixed on Mr. Brackstone, and then the game would be over for him, no matter what happened to her.

Mr. Brackstone could hear the same thing from his crouched position. He also realized his chances of getting away were growing very slim with each passing second. He dragged his wounded leg behind him through the dirt road and approached his escape route. Mr. Brackstone pulled up the heavy manhole cover to Riverside's sewage line. He hopped down into the large drainage pipe which was put in place to combat flooding around the river during the rainy season. He pulled the manhole cover back over his head, concealing his whereabouts from the outside world.

A large blue duffel bag was hanging from bungee cords off a nearby pipe just three feet from where the manhole opening was. Mr. Brackstone opened the bag frantically. He planned for such a day, if he should ever get desperate. Inside the bag, there was an air tank, some flippers, and a diver's mask. Mr. Brackstone put on his equipment quickly. He waddled backward to the end of the pipe and fell back into the murky Delaware River. Mr. Brackstone submerged beneath the murky water and began his perilous push for freedom.

Mildred followed the blood up to the manhole cover. She radioed into the chopper, giving them her location. She used all her strength to pull the heavy iron plate off. Then, she jumped into the pipe with her flashlight leading her weapon. Mildred saw the empty blue duffel bag crumpled up in the water. She walked to the end of the pipe and saw that the water was disturbed.

"Sky Bird, this is Agent Beron, our perp is in the water. I repeat, we have a fish on our hands. Switch to heat signature goggles and track him from this location, over."

"That is affirmative, Agent. We have your fish on our scanner, and we are tracking him. Holding for your instructions."

Mildred shot back through the manhole opening, only to be helped up by several Riverside police officers. They all ran to the bridge to get a better look at the situation. The chopper was hovering low over a fixed spot on the river. It slowly made its way along the water, following Mr. Brackstone's heat signature. Mildred smiled as she radioed in her next order.

"Sky Bird, do you have any shock grenades on board?"

"That is affirmative, Agent. We are loaded for swat on here."

"That is exactly what I wanted to hear, Sky Bird. Deploy grenades at a ten-second interval over our fish. He should find it hard to swim after that, over."

"Ten-four, Agent, we are deploying charges."

Mr. Brackstone could hear the chopper overhead, though underwater the blades sounded muffled and slow. He thought they were just searching the area like lost puppies, until he saw a plunge in the water ten yards in front of him. He halted his progress and watched the small canister float slowly toward the bottom of the murky Delaware. Then it exploded in a sudden burst of light and sound. The force hit Mr. Brackstone in the chest and sent him into an underwater cartwheel. He barely regained his composure and swam frantically toward the middle of the river, submerging as deep as he could. He heard another plunge behind him and raced to escape the impending blast. Another shock of light and sound hit Mr. Brackstone, this time from behind, forcing him down to the muddy bottom of the river. He slammed into the mud and lost his grip on his mouthpiece. The air bubbled out of the floating apparatus, revealing Mr. Brackstone's location to all onlookers above. He grabbed his mouthpiece and reapplied it, gasping for air. He pulled himself along the foggy bottom, hoping he could reach a depth that would hide him from his pursuers.

Mildred picked up her radio and ordered, "Sky Bird, you have him on the run. I want you to go to five-second intervals, and we should have our man in no time, over."

"That's a good idea, Agent. We will commence five-second drops. We are starting to lose his heat signature, however. He must be going as deep as he can down there, over."

"In that case, Sky Bird, I want you to dump all remaining charges in the area now, do you copy."

"Copy that, Agent, though I can't promise a healthy fish will float up."

"I'll take that chance, Sky Bird, over and out."

Mr. Brackstone flipped his skinny leg muscles with all his might, thrusting himself forward. He heard plunge after plunge, in front of him and behind him. He grabbed on to an old submerged log and braced for impact. The shock grenades went off unmercifully. The explosions sent water shooting twenty feet into the sky above the surface. On the river's bottom, Mr. Brackstone smashed against the muddy log, unable to hold his slipping grip.

He let go of the slimy log and struggled forward in an attempt to free himself from the blast radius, forcing his hands in front of him to clear the dust and dirt particles from the water. Mr. Brackstone lost his breath instantaneously, his eyes bulged out of his mask, and true fear struck the psychopath's black heart for the first time since his childhood. Floating in front of his quaking eyes, Mr. Brackstone came face-to-face with Eileen's decomposing severed head, half eaten by the wildlife with one eyeball hanging down her monstrous face. Her head must have been dislodged from its stone companion by one of the blasts. It floated ominously toward Mr. Brackstone's face, spinning around with loose slices of flesh fluttering off it.

Mr. Brackstone froze in disbelief. As the severed head unbelievably came within inches of his nose, a plunge echoed above his position. A metallic-green stun grenade floated downright next to Eileen's decapitated head. It exploded dramatically. The close proximity of the blast blinded Mr. Brackstone and knocked his face mask off. The powerful shock wave disintegrated Eileen's face. Mr. Brackstone reeled backward in an underwater somersault and began to unwillingly float to the unwelcoming surface.

There were law enforcement personnel from all reaches of the county scattered along the riverbank by now. Everyone saw the burst of bubbles that followed the last blast and trained their guns accordingly. Mildred ordered the chopper off at the first sight of Mr. Brackstone emerging from the depths of the turbulent Delaware

River. Every lawman, federal agent, and local deputy focused their weapons determinedly on Mr. Brackstone. He reared his head up, gasping for fresh air on the exposed surface. Mildred lifted up a bullhorn given to her by one of the local deputies.

"Mr. Clifford Brackstone, you are under arrest. Swim to the nearest shoreline and come out with your hands up."

Mr. Brackstone scanned the shores and saw that literally hundreds of guns waited for him to make the wrong move. This was it. The end of the story for Mr. Brackstone as far as he was concerned. He always thought in his twisted mind this moment would be something more poetic, something more deserving of his talents. He carefully waded in the water, looking up at Mildred standing proudly on the bridge in front of him. His black heart took control of him once again. He screamed out to his onetime victim, "I should have killed you all those years ago, Mildred. You should be the one in this river!"

Mildred picked up her bullhorn in rebuttal. "Yeah, well, I'm not. You are, however. I won't tell you again, Mr. Brackstone. There is no chance of escape. You are surrounded. Swim to the nearest shore, now!"

Mr. Brackstone squinted his evil eyes. The sun was just behind Mildred in the picturesque sky. He raised his hand to the surface of the water. Taking aim at Mildred's shadow in the sun, holding Barney's police-issued revolver, he fired a lone shot in a final attempt at taking his last victim. Mr. Brackstone's shot hit the iron pillar two inches to the left of Mildred's head. Before Mr. Brackstone could get off a second shot, a thundering rain of bullets plunged into the water and invaded his fatigued body. He convulsed repeatedly as each bullet struck his soft flesh and ripped hot lead holes through his submerged skin.

Even the sharpshooter fixed on the chopper opened fire on Mr. Brackstone, invading the air tank on his back. The tank exploded in a wild display of power. The firing stopped. When the water cleared, Mr. Brackstone's lifeless body rose to the surface, facedown in floating motionless sprawl. He had met his end in the very place he doomed his Nothing Girls to their final resting place.

Mildred looked on unconsciously, her senses dull to the moment. She did not know if she should feel happy or sad. Her entire life had led up to this moment. Though now that it was over, she somehow felt empty inside. No ticker tape parades, no glorious hoorays. Just a dead maniac gloomily floating in the Delaware River. The clock tower bells chimed twice in the background. Mr. Clifford Brackstone floated across the Delaware River toward the other side.

CHAPTER 35

Things to Be Said

THAT ISOLATED NIGHT, ST. PETER's Catholic Church held a vigil for the victims of Mr. Clifford Brackstone's hidden rampage. The news of the murders and subsequent events had already spread to every major media market in the tristate area. CNN trucks had already started to set up satellite links all over town. Mildred sat inside the first pew, kneeling in front of the old wooden altar, remembering the days when Father Conner used to console her.

A carved statue of Jesus soulfully looked down upon her. He seemed to look into her eyes with a somber gaze carved upon his face. It gave her a lasting sense that someone was on her side. Colette Jennings walked into the church amid a stir in the packed pews. Hundreds of cameras flashed behind her through the front door, but the media was barred from the ceremony. Huddled masses of hyena-like reporters shouted inappropriate questions at the young girl. She bravely walked through the front doors of the old suburban church and headed directly toward the podium.

As the doors closed, the church regained its calm. The glaring lights from the video cameras and the screaming voices dulled behind the huge wooden doors. The entire church fell silent. Mourning families and friends of the victims filled the pews and watched Colette struggle her way up to the main altar. She was covered in bandages. Word of what she had done to Mr. Brackstone had already spread like a gossip plague through the small town. Every memorial candle burned bright, illuminating her beautiful yet battered features as she stepped up to the altar. Father Conner's friend Father Pastore from the Delanco parish welcomed her with opened arms and a strong hug. He kissed the weeping youth on her forehead and begged her to be strong.

Colette approached the flat altar and touched the microphone, testing its sensitivity. The congregation looked on in a hushed anticipation and gave Colette their full attention. She wiped the tears from her bruised face and began a speech no child should ever have to make.

"Victims, family, friends, and heroes. This church holds all of these. We were all brought together in sorrow by one evil man who ripped the fabric of our small town. The wounds will heal one day, and Mr. Clifford Brackstone will become an old horror story to tell our children. But the scars will always remain. A single day will not go by when I won't think of Eileen, Mat, and Tom. They were true friends. They did not deserve to die so young or so brutally. All of the other victims should be remembered in our prayers. Though we cannot change what happened here, we can try to go on. Live our lives. I should be making a homecoming speech today. Instead, I have to say goodbye to three of the people I loved most in this world. Youth should never be overlooked. If someone had cared more years ago, we may have never had to witness this somber vigil. I ask that everyone in here learn a grave lesson from this. Protect your children. Not just the pretty ones or the strong ones. Protect the lonely, mistreated ones. Come together as a community, so this type of thing can never happen again. God gives us a gift when a child is born. I know you have all heard about what I did to stop Mr. Brackstone from taking me. I learned the price I will pay for that just today. I will never know that gift from God. I will never be able to have my own children."

The audience gasped. Colette's mother ran up to the altar at her side and embraced her.

"No, it's all right, Mother. I have to say this. We will all pay a price for what has happened here in Riverside. I plead and pray to all of you. Heed my words: do not allow innocence to be corrupted here ever again. As long as you live, make an effort to help the weak ones grow strong. God will judge us all on that. We live on a planet of innocence, and the unseen predator is king, if we allow him to remain unseen."

Colette's weeping mother helped her daughter to her seat. From the oldest women to the most masculine men, there was not a dry eye in the audience. Agent Branch sneaked into the church just moments after Colette had finished. He slid into the open seat next to Mildred.

"I think it's your turn to say something, Agent Beron."

"Hey, you're supposed to be in the hospital."

"I know, but I had a talk with the doctor, and he gave me a couple hours off to come join you. As long as I don't do anything too exciting…"

Mildred hugged Branch and kissed him on his cheek.

"I'm glad you could make it."

Branch coughed and held on to his bandaged abdomen.

"Hey, don't squeeze too hard, you might pop a stitch. Just get up there and speak your mind, Mildred. Tell them why you came here."

Mildred stood up and walked to the pulpit. Father Pastor announced her as she approached the microphone.

"This is Agent Mildred Beron, a former resident of Riverside and the person responsible for putting an end to Mr. Brackstone's evil deeds."

The parish stood up and clapped for Mildred, showing their appreciation for what their native daughter had accomplished.

"Please do not do that. Please sit down."

The parish did as she asked.

"I have a confession to make. I stand before all of you tonight a broken person. I am not a hero, or a savior. Many years ago, I, too, was a victim of Mr. Clifford Brackstone's malevolent hand. If I had the strength back then to say something, so many lives would have been spared. I cannot tell you how sorry I am for that. I know I was just a child. But, there is no excuse. Father Conner used to stand up here and tell a scattered few in his parish stories from the good book. I remember one very important verse that we should reflect on tonight. The story of Job. He was a man who had everything. When he was tested by God, when all of his things were taken from him to test his faith, he truly found the meaning of the Lord. This small town sits on the brink of that decision. All things have been taken from us. We are at the mercy of God. I believe in him. I know our lesson has been taught. I just hope we have listened to God and learned. There are so many people responsible for ending Mr. Brackstone's rampage through our town. I couldn't mention all of them. But, I would like to thank every one of the law enforcement personnel that put their lives on the line for this evil man to be brought to his ultimate justice. I would like to close with a passage. Psalm 1: 'Blessed is the man that walketh not in the council of the ungodly, nor standeth in the way of sinners, nor sitteth in the seat of the scornful. But his delight is in the law of the Lord, and in his law doth he meditate day and night. And he shall be like a tree planted by the rivers of water, that bringeth forth his fruit in his season, his leaf also shall not wither, and whatsoever he doeth shall prosper. The ungodly are not so but are like chaff which the wind driveth away. Therefore the ungodly shall not stand in judgment, nor sinners in the congregation of the righteous. For the Lord knoweth the way of the righteous, but the way of the ungodly shall perish.'"

Mildred looked up from the Bible, tightly grasping Father Conner's rosary beads, and continued.

"Mr. Clifford Brackstone has perished. His story will fade in the wind. Let us stand strong in the water of the river and give thanks to God that this nightmare is over."

CHAPTER 36

Doorways

A SHADOWY GRAY ROOM RESTED cold and lifeless in the basement of the Whiteside Funeral Home. An immense freezer door creaked open; cold, smoky claws leaped out into the warm air and dissipated instantaneously. A low swinging florescent light showed the dullest effects of a somber death chamber. Mr. Brackstone's father pushed himself out of the freezer and toiled with his son's heavy body cart. The old sightless ghoul managed his way to the ancient embalming station. He pulled a bloody white sheet off Mr. Brackstone's bullet-riddled corpse.

Mr. Brackstone's naked body lay cold and stiff on the chilly metal slab. His mouth gaped open, exposing his snarled yellow teeth. His powder-white skin seemed to be invaded with ice-blue veins spidering across his lifeless body. His empty eyes still had the deadly, captured look of ultimate astonishment. One by one, the old man meticulously removed the mangled metal bullets from Mr. Brackstone's cadaver, plunking them into a large metal bucket underneath the table. The sound of the dropping bullets against flimsy tin racked the old man's nerves. His unpleasant, blood-soaked hands shook feverously from mounting anxiety. The blind mortician began to cry through his hazy eyes, whimpering to himself like an injured dog. His psyche felt bewildered thinking of his departed child.

He courageously sucked up his pride. Then, he slipped off his extra-large white overcoat and threw it into the corner of the gray room. Solemnly looking down at Mr. Brackstone's stiff corpse, he uttered, "You did a fine job, son. You did everything just the way I taught you to do it. Don't worry, we still have a chance to get you out of this mess. It's not too late. It's not too late."

The lurking specter covered Mr. Brackstone's lower half with some old blankets and put his heavy head under a flat pillow. He opened Mr. Brackstone's mouth and placed a square wooden block between each side of his back teeth. As fast as the old man's body could take him, he hurried over to the nearest electrical outlet and plugged in a bright-orange extension cord into the wall. He ran back over to Mr. Brackstone and took the other end of the cord and exposed the naked ends of the wires. He shoved one end into a bullet hole near Mr. Brackstone's heart and the other end in a bullet hole at the bottom of his rib cage.

"Here we go, son. Like I always told you, the strong will survive. If you are one of the strong ones, you will live again. You will help me cleanse this putrid town of the fainthearted. I can't keep it up alone. Come back to me, Clifford. Come back to your teacher, to your father, to your master!"

The old man madly flipped the power switch on the wall, and Mr. Brackstone's body convulsed wildly. It flexed and jumped on the metal slab, making an awful clanging sound of wet flesh on cold metal. He turned the switch off and ran over to Mr. Brackstone's body. No pulse. He hustled back over to the switch and hit Mr. Brackstone with another heavy current. Steam began to rise from Mr. Brackstone's open bullet holes as his body flailed around on the table out of control. He turned the power off once again and ran over to his son. He placed his finger on Mr. Brackstone's wrist and pressed firmly.

"Live Clifford, live! You have not finished your work yet, son. Live and complete what you have started here. Wake up and take your place at my side, at the top of food chain!"

Just then, his aged finger felt a slight bump. But no more beats followed. His crazed face rejected the bitter truth that lay motionless in front of him. He shuffled back to the wall and hit the power switch again. Mr. Brackstone's lifeless corpse danced wildly across the metal tabletop. Small flames began to rise from his open bullet holes. The horrible smell of burning flesh rushed over the room, assuring the old blind man there was nothing else he could do.

*****

Mr. Brackstone saw nothing but darkness. He felt at peace with himself. Shots of distant lightning cracked around him but stopped quickly. A rush of wind hurried past him, and he found himself in a small room facing two colossal doors. He inspected them briefly and noticed the doorknobs were so large he could not hope to reach or turn them.

"What do you think is behind them?" a child's voice asked from the dark corner of the room.

"Who is it? Show yourself!" Mr. Brackstone demanded.

Slowly, a very frail eleven-year-old Mr. Clifford Brackstone emerged from the dark shadow of the corner. The young boy was dressed in nothing but his white briefs and shivered with every ensuing step.

"My name is Clifford," the young boy said.

The newly deceased Mr. Brackstone looked on in astonishment. He could not believe he was standing next to a young version of himself. As he inspected the young boy, he noticed that he, too, was dressed in nothing but a snug set of white underwear.

"Clifford, how long have you been here?"

The young boy shrugged his shoulders in confusion.

"I don't know how long it's been. I know it has been a long time though. I feel like I've been here waiting for something. Now it has finally come."

"What have you been waiting for, Clifford?"

Young Mr. Clifford Brackstone put his finger across his lips.

"Shh. It's coming. Can't you hear it? From behind the doors, listen."

They both stood in front of the doors, motionless. Listening to muffled sounds pounding through the door, Mr. Brackstone was beginning to get scared. He turned to his younger version and demanded an answer.

"What is coming, Clifford? Tell me what we are waiting for."

The young boy looked up and spoke, "Judgment. We are waiting for judgment."

Cold, intangible fear filled Mr. Brackstone's heart. Small tears trickled down his cold face and fell onto his bullet-riddled body. He reached down and touched the holes in his chest. A small bit of smoke trickled out, and burning pain began to radiate through the wounds.

"Do they hurt?" young Clifford asked as he looked sadly at his older version.

"Yeah, they hurt really bad."

"Maybe it will stop. Hey, listen, I can hear something through my door. It's getting closer, whatever it is."

The young boy walked closer to the door closest to him. Mr. Brackstone went to stop him but was frozen in place. His entire body locked up, and he wasn't able to move a muscle. The large doorknob began to turn slowly. Loud howls began to bellow through the door and into the small room. Mr. Brackstone called out to his younger version.

"Get away from there. Run as fast as you can. Get away, goddamn it!"

The door began to open. A bright light radiated from behind the cracks of the archway. It temporarily blinded Mr. Brackstone. As he regained his sight, he witnessed a wonderful scene. Standing in the open doorway, just a couple of feet away from his frozen body, was his old friend Sam. The mighty German shepherd raced into the room and jumped up onto young Clifford's chest. They embraced, and Sam happily licked his young master's face. The boy laughed hysterically. Mr. Brackstone screamed out from his frozen pose.

"Over here! Sam, I'm over here!"

Sam paid him no attention. The young boy looked over to Mr. Brackstone, and his smile dropped off his face dramatically.

"I'm sorry. This is for me. You have to wait for your judgment."

Sam and Clifford pounced through the bright, cascading doorway as it shut abruptly behind them, leaving Mr. Brackstone frozen in the darkness alone, aimlessly waiting in front of his door. Darkness enclosed the room. Mr. Brackstone looked at the ominous door with quaking eyes. Days seemed to pass by as he remained in his frozen dementia. Then suddenly, he heard a familiar noise from behind his door.

Mr. Brackstone listened more intently. He concentrated so hard on picking up the sound again he could hear his own heavy breaths. Like a dreaded, recurring nightmare you cannot run from, the sound rained through his eardrums again—the horrible, ungodly sound of his mother's feet dragging down the hallway toward his door.

He uttered to himself in disbelief, "No…it can't be…"

The End

About the Author

BILL DUFF IS A GRADUATE of the University of Tennessee and former professional football player and television host of the History channel *Human Weapon*. Bill is married to Ms. Jenifer Duff, a psychological therapist whose sobering stories were the catalyst and inspiration for much of his first novel *Meet Mr. Brackstone*.

Bill is a native of Southern New Jersey by the great Delaware River but now makes his home on the sleepy shores of southern Maryland.

CPSIA information can be obtained
at www.ICGtesting.com
Printed in the USA
LVHW032116060420
652381LV00003B/285

9 781646 284337